"What aren't you saying, Bailey?"

Ed stepped closer so he could see the truth in her eyes.

Something flashed there again. Fear? Defiance?

"We're not in this together, you know," she finally muttered. "I was doing just fine here before you showed up."

He stepped closer. "Were you?"

"I've always done things on my own. I just decided to take matters into my own hands and see if the intruder was still here."

He didn't buy her story for a second. "And was he?"

She swallowed so hard that her throat muscles visibly tightened. "You didn't see him. Did you?"

He shifted, his hands going to his hips. "You need to tell me what kind of game you're playing. Otherwise, we might both end up dead."

Wrinkles appeared at the corner of her eyes. "Look, I'm sorry. I won't wander away again. I had a moment of bad judgment."

That little excuse wasn't going to settle with him. But she wasn't saying anything else right now.

He'd keep an eye on her. He didn't trust her.

But for now, they had to work together.

Christy Barritt's books have won a Daphne du Maurier Award for Excellence in Suspense and Mystery and have been twice nominated for the RT Reviewers' Choice Award. She's married to her Prince Charming, a man who thinks she's hilarious—but only when she's not trying to be. Christy's a self-proclaimed klutz, an avid music lover and a road trip aficionado. For more information, visit her website at christybarritt.com.

Books by Christy Barritt

Love Inspired Suspense

Keeping Guard
The Last Target
Race Against Time
Ricochet
Desperate Measures
Hidden Agenda

The Security Experts Series

Key Witness
Lifeline
High-Stakes Holiday Reunion

Visit the Author Profile page at Harlequin.com

HIDDEN AGENDA

CHRISTY BARRITT

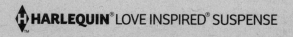

HARLEQUIN® LOVE INSPIRED® SUSPENSE

Recycling programs
for this product may
not exist in your area.

LOVE INSPIRED BOOKS

ISBN-13: 978-0-373-44656-8

Hidden Agenda

Copyright © 2015 by Christy Barritt

www.Harlequin.com

Printed in U.S.A.

Do not conform to the pattern of this world,
but be transformed by the renewing of your mind.
Then you will be able to test and approve what God's will is—
his good, pleasing and perfect will.
—Romans 12:2

This book is dedicated to the
unseen and unrecognized defenders of freedom.

ONE

Bailey Williams froze, the page from her novel half-turned and candlelight dancing across the words. The book slipped from her hands. Instead of retrieving it, she pulled the blanket tighter across her shoulders.

What was that sound?

The raging storm outside had already toppled some large tree branches into the yard. Power had gone out more than three hours ago, and the nighttime—deep and blinding—had fallen in the blink of an eye.

She was supposed to leave today, but there'd been no boats coming or going from Smuggler's Cove. So she was stuck here, in this huge old house, on a creepy island in the middle of a subtropical storm.

Could things get any worse?

She squeezed her eyes shut as she remembered the events of the past several days. Events that included losing one of the best employers she'd ever had. That involved losing the job she'd held for the past eight months. That comprised the prospect of starting over again. Going somewhere new. Finding another job.

Mr. Carter had died a week ago today. She'd stuck around, trying to get his affairs in order. She'd planned his funeral, cleaned his house and prepared food for guests who'd come into town.

She felt like the only family the man had, yet she wasn't

family. She was simply Mr. Carter's nurse, someone who helped on occasion with meals and housework and offered a listening ear. She mourned the man as if she'd been his daughter. In a way, the man had come to feel like a second father.

Another crash sounded, and her lungs tightened. What was that? Had the wind sent something toppling into the house? Had one of the shutters come loose?

She tugged the blanket even tighter around her shoulders. The October day had already been frigid before the power had gone out, the heat along with it. She'd tried to start a fire but had been unsuccessful.

Reaching into the drawer of the table beside the padded chair in her bedroom, she grabbed a flashlight. She flicked the switch to the on position. The light waned, blinked, flickered, but finally shone brightly.

Thank goodness. At least *that* was working in her favor.

As soon as the thought entered her mind, the flashlight went black, the room along with it. A draft must have whispered extinction orders across the candle that burned on the table beside her chair. Two lights in two seconds—it was a double whammy of darkness.

Bailey hit the flashlight against her palm. Tapped the top of the light. Shook the batteries back and forth.

The sweet beacon of illumination wouldn't come back on.

Perfect. She frowned.

She was going to have to check out the sound, whether she wanted to or not. She couldn't simply stay in her old bedroom, huddled on the big, comfy chair until the storm passed. For more than one reason. Buckets of rain could be flooding into the house. The bay could have climbed the shores, reaching the porch, in which case she'd need to evacuate. For all she knew, this whole island could be in danger of washing away. The place seemed like little more than a sandbar anyway. Or what if lightning struck nearby, started a fire even? There were so many things that could go wrong, so many reasons not to stay in her room hiding.

Her throat constricted as she stepped into the dark hallway that snaked through the east wing of the estate. She thought her eyes would have adjusted to the darkness by now, but not even a hint of light reached the interior of the house, especially not right here.

In broad daylight, the place was spooky. On a stormy night, it was terrifying.

She first thought about going downstairs. But the idea caused hazy fear to engulf her, making her feel lightheaded and unsteady. She changed course and hurried in the opposite direction, away from the massive staircase that led to the front door and instead toward the door at the end of the hallway.

She passed one closed door. Two. Three.

Each one made her tense, made worst-case scenarios flash through her mind like a broken reel from a horror flick. Images of people hiding. Madmen lurking. Danger awaiting.

Her walk turned into a run. She reached the end of the hallway, her destination. Her hands trembled on the doorknob, but finally she managed to twist it.

The moment she threw open the door, purple light flashed from the alcove upstairs. Her heart raced.

Lightning. Just lightning.

No figures lurked in the shadows.

Maybe she shouldn't have been reading that mystery novel earlier. The story had put too many spooky ideas into her head.

Before she could second-guess herself, her fingers gripped the iron handles of the spiral staircase that twisted upward to the widow's walk. Bailey would have a bird's-eye view from there of anything going on outside. Floods. Fires. Downed trees.

She rushed up the steps at a dizzying pace until she reached the enclosed landing up top. The stretch was narrow with windows on each side. There was only one bench and a lonely spider plant. She usually liked to come up here alone, especially when she needed to think. Right now, it would serve as a lookout.

Still clutching the blanket around her shoulders, she took her first step.

The only time she could catch a glimpse of anything in the darkness was when lightning lit the sky. The first strike showed her the Chesapeake Bay. Angry waves roiled there, charging forward before beating against the sandy beaches of the island. The second strike showed her several massive tree branches that now littered the yard.

Where had that crash come from earlier? Had a window broken from the gale-force gusts outside? Had a tree fallen onto the garage? Blown the pier away?

Speaking of which, maybe being up here wasn't the best idea. Not with this storm raging. All she needed was for the wind to make a projectile of one of those live oak trees lining the walk leading to the front door. She'd be a goner, and it would be her own doing.

Thunder shook the cool, water-dimpled windowpanes. As Bailey stood there, the glass rattled as the deep sound rumbled and rumbled some more. The growl reached all the way to her bones.

When lightning flashed again, something beside the house caught her eye. Her heart leaped into her throat with enough force to jostle her entire body.

Was that…a man?

She stepped closer to the glass and wiped away some of the fog there. She couldn't have seen that correctly. Her eyes were playing tricks on her.

She blinked, waiting and holding her breath to get a glimpse of the back of the house again.

The next time the sky lit, Bailey saw him. A man stood at the back door, his fists pounding against the wood. She didn't have to hear the knocks to know they were forceful, almost angry.

He was trying to get inside, she realized.

Desperate to get inside, for that matter.

The only reason someone would want to get in here was to start trouble. Mr. Carter had said some cryptic things in his final days. He'd spoken of someone coming here and destroying people. He'd urged Bailey to protect his things.

She'd thought Mr. Carter had been delusional. But what if there was more to his words? What if in his last moments he'd finally spoken the truth? Though a pleasant and friendly man, he'd been so private, so selective in what he shared.

With the force of a bolt of electricity, Bailey realized that she had to get down from here before the man at the back door saw her.

Just as she took a step back, the man lifted his head.

Looked right at her.

Even with the distance between them, Bailey felt the anger in the man's gaze.

A black cloak fell outside again, and the man disappeared.

The next instance, the sky filled with light again.

Just in time for her to see the stranger kick the door open.

Bailey had to hide, she realized. Now. It was only a matter of time before the intruder found her.

Ed Carter saw the figure on the widow's walk. For a moment—and just a moment—he thought he'd seen a ghost. Not that he believed in ghosts. But the woman had looked so eerie, especially with the blanket around her shoulders and the sullen look on her face.

Then he realized an intruder was lurking in the house.

In his dad's house.

Could she be the same person who'd killed his father? That was his best guess. Maybe she'd stuck around, using some kind of alias as she tried to stake claim to his father's fortune. Money made people do crazy things, like declaring to be long-lost relatives. For all he knew, his father had gotten remarried—to the wrong woman. As crazy as that sounded, it was the best-case scenario.

The worst-case scenario was that his father had brought classified information here. Information that people wanted. The *wrong* people wanted and would do anything to get their hands on.

Ed intended to put an end to all of this. Now.

Ed knew the truth. Despite his father's congestive heart failure, he had not died of natural causes, and Ed would prove it.

He forgot about formalities and about trying to preserve his dad's house. All thoughts of coming home and paying respects to his dad, of both mourning and celebrating his dad's life, disappeared.

With expert training, he kicked the door. Wood splintered from the hinges, revealing the inside of the house. His years in the CIA had taught him a few things.

More than he would have liked sometimes.

He stared at the blackness oozing from the interior. It was thick, almost as though the darkness was a material thing.

He reached for the light switch. The electricity was out. Of course.

A storm like this could literally wipe out the whole island and send it toppling into the bay. Not to mention what it could do for the power grid of the small, isolated community.

As if to confirm his theory, lightning slashed the sky behind him, followed by a loud rumble of thunder. This storm was a beast.

He'd barely made it to the island in time. The pilot he'd hired was an expert. The storm came on faster than anticipated, and they'd landed just before the squall unleashed at full force. If his pilot hadn't been so experienced, the plane would have probably crashed in the high winds and massive downpour.

Ed had waited inside the tiny, two-room airport for a break in the weather before traveling the island roads, which were only accessible by golf cart or bike. A man at the airport had informed him that the bridge leading to his father's estate was treacherous with the rising tide.

But after a couple of hours of waiting, Ed had decided to take his chances. Alvin, the town chauffeur, had agreed to give him a ride to the bridge in a covered golf cart and bring Ed's luggage for him later. Meanwhile, his pilot chose to camp out at the airport so he could leave as soon as the storm passed.

Once Ed had waded through the water and reached the house, he'd discovered that his key to his dad's place no longer worked.

In the storm, the place looked even creepier than Ed remembered. It was a Georgian-style mansion with towers on the sides and a widow's walk stretching across the roof. A shipping captain had built the place after staking claim to a good portion of land on the island nearly a century ago.

As the eerily silent house surrounded him, Ed remembered the figure on the widow's walk. He didn't have any time to waste.

He shook some water off himself and reached under his coat to retrieve his handgun, turning on the penlight on top so he'd have some light. In his line of work, one could never be too careful.

Moving slowly, carefully, he stepped deeper into the house.

He scanned the kitchen. There was no sign of movement. He doubted the woman would have been able to get from the widow's walk down here in that short amount of time.

Where had she gone? Had she hidden? Tried to escape?

He wasn't sure. But he was going to find out.

Locating the woman in a house this massive, with so many twists and turns and back hallways, would be difficult. He'd start by going to the second level, and then he'd travel toward the staircase leading toward the widow's walk.

He walked slowly, daring any of the wooden steps to creak and announce his presence. If he'd learned one thing through the years, it was how to be quiet and stealthy, how to be light on his feet and disappear into the shadows.

He reached the hallway and headed to the right. A long line of doors waited there, each a potential trap. He kept his gun drawn and his steps steady. He reached the first door and pushed it open.

An empty bedroom stared back at him.

He did the same at the next two doors.

At the fourth door, he paused when he saw the edge of a blanket on the floor.

He turned and spotted a woman behind the door. *The* woman. With a lamp above her head, poised like a baseball bat.

"I don't think so," she mumbled, starting to swing.

In one swift motion, he slid his gun back into the holster and grabbed her arm—just in time to stop her from crashing the ceramic base on his head. He squeezed her wrist until the lamp shattered onto the floor. The woman gasped, her eyes widening with surprise and fear. He still didn't let go of her. No telling what she would try next.

"Are you crazy?" He kept his voice low and serious, refusing to break his gaze. If anything, he knew how to handle himself in tense situations.

The woman, at one moment frozen, suddenly came to life. She struggled against him, twisting, turning and trying to get away.

"Get your hands off me!" she growled.

She was a fighter. He'd give her credit for having spunk. But he did this for a living.

Based on the way she flailed, this woman was no trained assassin. She probably hadn't even taken any self-defense classes, for that matter. But who was she? As far as he knew, this place was supposed to be empty. Of course, he'd been out of touch for the past several months, on an assignment that required deep cover.

The woman still tried to jerk away from him.

"Calm down," he muttered.

"Don't tell me to calm down!"

He pinned both of her arms behind her back and restrained her until she stopped struggling. Her eyes didn't lose their fight, though.

He locked gazes with her. "Who are you and what are you doing here?"

She tried to jerk away one more time. "I should be asking you the same thing."

Ed sighed, waiting for her to wear herself out. "I'm not in the mood for guessing games, so why don't you answer my question?"

"Why don't *you* let me go? Then maybe we can talk."

He wanted to really see her eyes, wanted to see if there was truth or deceit in their depths when she answered. It was a calculated risk he needed to take. He released her hand and pulled out his gun in one swift motion.

"Back up to the wall," he ordered. "Slowly. Don't make any sudden moves or you'll regret it."

She slowly turned, took two steps back and stood stiffly against the flowered wallpaper.

He shined the light atop his gun on the woman, wanting to get a good look at her. She was on the taller side. Slim. Had long hair, light brown and straight, that fell halfway down her back. He couldn't tell what color her eyes were—probably brown, he guessed—but they were big with thick lashes.

He'd been deceived by more than one pretty woman in his day, enough that he was now immune to batting eyelashes and sweet smiles.

"Start talking." With mild amusement, he added, "Please."

The woman raised her hands, her chest heaving with shallow breaths. "I'm not looking for trouble. As soon as the storm is over, I'll be gone from here. None of this stuff is mine, but I think you're deplorable if you're going to steal from a dead man."

"Steal?" He raised an eyebrow, curious now.

"Yes, of course steal." Suddenly, the woman pressed herself harder into the wall and rubbed her throat. "If you're not a thief, then why are you here?"

Seeing her fear caused something to click in his mind. While he didn't want to be manipulated by a woman, he never wanted to see a woman look that frightened. He especially never wanted to be the cause of that fear.

"Look, I'm not going to hurt you." To prove it, he put his gun away, tucking it safely into its holster under his sopping wet jacket. "I just wasn't expecting anyone to be here."

"Believe me. Neither was I. I wasn't even expecting to be here." She shivered as thunder rumbled through the house again. "Especially not in this storm."

"Maybe we should start over." He extended his hand, still cautious and on guard, but some of his edge leaving him after her comment about his dad. "I'm Ed."

She stared at his hand a moment before reaching forward. Her grip felt tentative, uncertain. She still didn't trust him. Smart woman.

"I'm Bailey. I was Mr. Carter's nurse up until the time he died a week ago. I stayed around trying to take care of his affairs, since he had no family around to do so."

He heard the undercurrents of judgment in her voice. "He had no family close by, huh?"

Her eyes flickered with emotion. "Just a good-for-nothing son, who never visited. Not even for his father's funeral." Her words sounded protective and loyal—and judgmental.

"His son sounds like a lousy excuse for a human being." Ed kept his voice light, tried to disguise the hurt there. He was the master of disguising how he felt. Years of working undercover did that to a person.

"I agree. I would have done anything to spend more time with my own father before he died. Family should be there for each other." Her voice cracked.

"You're right. Family should be there for each other."

She eyed him suspiciously. "And why exactly are *you* here, Ed?"

He raised his chin. "Because this is my house now, and I intend on finding out who killed my father."

TWO

Bailey stared at the man in front of her.

This was Mr. Carter's son? The hotshot lawyer from DC who never came to visit his father? Who couldn't even make it to his funeral because of "pressing business"?

She didn't know the man, and already she didn't like him. She didn't have to know him to know his type. He was career-oriented, into the social scene, all about climbing ladders—socially, professionally and financially. People weren't on his priority list or on his radar, for that matter. He only cared if they helped him advance in some way.

"I'm glad you could finally make it," she finally muttered.

Suddenly, she wasn't scared anymore, just annoyed. Why did this man think he could come traipsing in here after being absent from his father's life for so long?

Probably because he realized his father's last will and testament would be read soon. Ed most likely wanted what was left of his father's fortune. That fit the image she'd developed of the good-for-nothing son.

In the darkness, she could only make out the outline of the man. She could tell that he was tall, that his shoulders were broad. He was wet from the rain, and the moisture brought with it the scent of woodsy cologne. She'd guess, based on Mr. Carter's age and the sound of the man's voice, that Ed was in his midthirties.

Strangely enough, Mr. Carter didn't keep any pictures of his son here at the house. There were plenty of pictures of Mr. Carter's wife, who'd died eight years ago. But none of his son. Bailey had always thought it was odd. She'd asked Mr. Carter about it once, and he'd only said that his son didn't like his picture to be taken.

At that moment, Ed stepped closer. She could feel the coldness of his icy gaze. "I don't have to explain myself to you."

She raised her chin, not ready to back down. Someone had to stand up for Mr. Carter. Ed hadn't been around to do it. "No, but it's too bad your dad isn't here anymore so you could explain things to him."

His tone became even cooler. "My dad understood."

She raised her chin higher, questioning for a moment whether she should be so hard on the man. She realized this was none of her business, that she'd simply been hired help. But how could a son not be there for his father in his dying days? How could he have missed the funeral?

And what was all of this talk about finding the person who'd killed his father? Was that just some kind of front to distract her from his real intentions? His selfish intentions?

She lowered her chin, trying to rein in her emotions, which seemed to be spinning out of control tonight, right along with her imagination. "Your father died of heart failure. You're mistaken if you think someone killed him. You must have gotten faulty information."

"I'm in the business of information." He stepped closer. Even in the dark, she saw his glare.

She'd gotten on his bad side, and rightfully so. But she didn't care. She was leaving here as soon as this storm cleared, and she'd never see this man again. At the moment, she wasn't worried about impressing anyone, especially not Ed Carter.

She stepped closer, close enough to show that she wasn't

one to back down from a confrontation. "If you're in the business of information, then you need to check your sources. I was with your father when he died."

Ed didn't break his gaze. "Then that makes you my number one suspect."

She sucked in a deep breath, outrage bursting inside her. "You think that I—"

Just then, a crash sounded downstairs.

Ed and Bailey's eyes met and, for a moment, they seemed to agree. Something was wrong. Seriously wrong.

And standing here arguing would do nothing to help figure out what.

Ed's muscles tightened when he heard the noise.

He'd hoped to handle one catastrophe at a time.

Now, instead of trying to figure what in the world this woman was talking about, he had to investigate the source of that shattered glass.

If he were less of a gentleman, he might leave this Bailey woman up here to defend herself. But he wasn't that kind of guy. No matter how frustrating the woman might be, she was coming with him.

"Stay close," he ordered.

She crossed her arms, her gaze defiant and stubborn. "I'd rather take my chances alone."

"This is no time to be difficult." He should just leave her. If only his conscience would let him.

"I'm not being difficult. I'm being honest."

The woman had guts. But he spoke the truth—this wasn't the time to try out her hand at independence. She was his first suspect in his father's death, but he'd learned a thing or two about having tunnel vision in his line of work. Until he had more information, he would keep his eyes open for others. He didn't have enough evidence to make a case against any one person yet.

"Stay with me," he repeated. He turned, tired of wasting time. He needed to check out that sound.

When he was sure that Bailey was right behind him, he moved toward the stairs. He kept his gun raised, waiting for any sound or sign of approaching danger. Nothing gave any indication that someone else was in the house.

The crash could have been caused by the storm. But until he knew for sure, Ed had to explore every possibility. There were an uncountable number of people out there who'd like to kill Ed or who could have killed his father. Danger was like breathing for Ed—it was a given. He was always on guard. Always suspicious. It was a hard way to live, but he'd gotten used to it—until recently. Something was shifting inside him, and he wasn't sure what or how to handle it.

Despite her bravado earlier, Bailey stayed surprisingly close behind him. He could hear her breaths coming quick and fast. Though he suspected she would never admit it, she was scared.

He stopped at the base of the stairs, and Bailey collided with him. He pivoted in time to see her toppling backward. He grabbed her arm and steadied her before she hurt herself. When he released her, she brushed her shirt off. Getting rid of his touch maybe?

He didn't have time for these games.

He put a finger over his lips to signal silence. She nodded and stayed behind him as they stepped into the kitchen. Wind swept through the room, bringing a chill with it. As lightning flashed again, the ragged edges of one of the bay windows by the breakfast nook came into view.

A tree limb lay half inside, half outside the house.

He let out the breath he'd been holding. The noise had just been nature doing the damage, not anyone dangerous. He lowered his gun.

"It looks like it was the storm after all," Bailey muttered, stepping out from behind him, her shoulders relaxing some. "A nuisance, but the better of the options racing through my mind. I'll get a broom."

He tucked his weapon into his jacket. "Know where any plastic is? I need to cover that hole up."

"Look in the west wing of the house. There are entire rooms with furniture covered in sheets of the stuff. You should be able to find something there."

Her words were cold. She thought she knew him, knew his reasons for being away. But she had no idea. And he didn't have to explain himself to her. In fact, he *wouldn't* explain himself to her. All of this was none of her business.

He'd come here to figure out who'd killed his dad. He only wished he had more to go on than the cryptic message his father's friend had left him. Then the man had died before relaying any information. Now his father was dead, as well.

As Ed headed into the blackness known as the west wing, he comforted himself with the fact that his father had run a check on Bailey before she was hired. But the best operatives were good. Really good. They slipped by the normal screenings. A few had slipped by high-level screenings.

Until he could identify the guilty party, he'd trust no one.

He was no fool. When his father had told him he was hiring a nurse, Ed had looked into Bailey himself. Her past had seemed seriously lacking. Could that be a sign she was a Goody Two-shoes or that her background had been fabricated?

He stopped at the first room in the hallway. The door creaked open. On the other side, he saw what was probably a ballroom at one time. Pieces of furniture stood like pretend ghosts in a haunted house. Each was covered and draped with either plastic or white sheets.

He grabbed some thick plastic off a wing chair and carried it back into the kitchen. Bailey was already there sweeping up the glass shards on the floor.

"Nails?" he asked.

He didn't have to see her expression to know her thoughts. *If you'd been around more, maybe you wouldn't have to ask me these questions.*

He wished he had been around more. He'd wanted to be. But his job had required a lot of him. In essence, it had required his life, and Ed's father knew that. Ed's father had helped him get the position. His dad knew all about the risks, the sacrifices. It came with the territory.

Bailey continued to brush the glass into a trash can. "The toolbox is under the sink."

While he was gone, Bailey had lit some candles around the room. Warm light flickered at the sink, on the breakfast table and on top of the kitchen island.

Ed found the nails and a hammer—right where Bailey had said they would be—and, after moving the limb from the window, he secured the thick plastic around the frame. At least the room would be protected against water damage. It wouldn't do much to keep intruders out, though. There was little he could do about that now.

While he had the toolbox, he also hammered the back door shut. Bailey watched him, her arms crossed and eyes suspicious. Finally, Ed stepped back and looked at his work. It was nothing to write home about, but it would do. In the morning, he'd see if he could find the supplies to fix the door.

"I'll put those tools up for you," Bailey offered.

Before he could insist that he could do it, she grabbed the hammer. Their hands brushed, and his heart jolted with electricity. He cleared his throat, brushing off his surprise. "Your hands are ice-cold. Do you have any firewood? We need to get some heat in this place."

She turned, squatting to return the hammer to its location under the sink. "Yes. A fire would be great. I wasn't successful at starting one myself."

At least the lack of a fire wasn't an effort to conceal her presence here. "It's going to get cold, and the storm isn't supposed to let up anytime soon," he finally said. "It looks like both of us are stuck here for a while."

She stood up and offered what looked like a forced smile. "So it appears."

He walked into the living room, a grand space with a ceiling two stories high, ornate bookcases stretching the height of the walls, and various seating areas where people could nestle down and catch up.

Too bad there would be no nestling down and no catching up.

He slid his wet coat off, grateful that his clothes underneath were still dry. Then he grabbed some logs and put them on the hearth. He balled up some newspaper he'd found on the floor to use for kindling. Bailey stood close, watching his every move, and finally handed him some matches.

He watched as the paper caught flame. Something about the moment reminded him of how very alone he was now. Both parents dead. No brothers or sisters. No family of his own. There was nothing waiting for him if he left the CIA. Nothing.

"Your father always liked to make fires himself," Bailey muttered, her voice breaking him from his thoughts. "He never let me help."

Ed stepped back, waiting for the flames to come to life. "Sounds like my dad."

He glanced at Bailey. Had he heard sorrow in the woman's voice? She stood there with the sleeves of her sweatshirt pulled over her hands. Her arms were crossed over her chest and her eyes downcast, almost sad. Maybe all of this defensiveness was because Bailey truly did care about his father. He didn't have time to ponder it now.

A moment later, the fire hissed, yawned and finally roared to life. Bailey stepped closer and rubbed her hands together. Orange light danced across her face.

Her very pleasant face.

Not that it mattered to Ed. He squatted there, mesmerized by the flames for another moment.

After a few minutes, Bailey stepped back. Her gaze narrowed as she looked at something in the distance.

Then she froze. Sucked in a quick breath. Stepped back.

Ed sprang to his feet, tense and ready for action. "What is it?"

Her wide eyes met his. "You came in through the back door, right?"

"That's correct."

She pointed toward the front door. "Then who left those wet footprints there?"

Bailey grabbed the fire poker and wrapped her fingers firmly around the handle. If there was someone else in this house, she was going to be prepared to fight him or her. Right beside Ed.

She didn't think Ed was the most upstanding guy, but she also didn't think he'd harm her.

Unless he continued to suspect she had something to do with his father's death.

Which was absurd.

Just then, Ed turned from scanning the room. He looked back at her, and she sucked in another deep breath.

The firelight revealed the intricacies of his face.

Startling blue eyes, thick dark hair, perfectly proportioned features. He had a slight scar under his right eye and a small dimple at his chin.

It would have been better if Bailey had remained in

the dark about how he looked. At least that way, in her mind, the man would have remained an ogre. Instead, he was good-looking enough for Hollywood. But his looks only added to her initial impression that he was shallow and superficial.

"Were you expecting anyone else?" Ed asked, pulling out his gun.

Bailey shook her head. "No one. Not even you."

"Anyone else have a key?"

"No. Not even you, apparently." She bit her lip. She really had to get control of her tongue and stop spouting off everything that came into her mind.

"Mine doesn't work anymore. Thank you," he added with a touch of sarcasm. "I might also add that *I* had a key and you didn't know about it. There could be others."

Bailey's mind raced through the possibilities. "If someone else was here, why didn't they announce their entrance?"

"Maybe he or she didn't realize you were here. The door's intact. No one broke it down in order to get inside." He reached for his gun. "Stay here."

"That's a switch from your earlier order to stay with you."

He scowled. "I'm trying not to get you killed."

"And earlier?"

He sighed. "We could stand here and argue all day. I'd feel better if I followed the footsteps just in case there's someone less than honorable waiting at the end of the trail."

"And I'd feel better if I carried my weight." She still didn't trust the man, but she'd come to find a certain amount of security in his presence, even in the short amount of time since they'd met. As thunder rumbled again, she gripped the poker tighter. "No way am I staying here by myself."

It had seemed like a good idea earlier, when she was up in the hallway and feeling stubborn. But now that she knew someone else was definitely here, the thought of being alone seemed terrifying.

He stared at her another moment before shrugging. "Fine. Suit yourself. But be careful."

She shivered. They couldn't blame those footprints on the wind or the storm, as she'd done with the other calamities around the place. No, someone had clearly been here. Recently.

Ed bent toward the footprints and began following them through the living room, down the east wing.

Bailey stayed behind Ed. Near enough to touch him. Scared enough that she wanted to grab ahold of his jacket.

But she wouldn't do that.

He followed the trail. Out of the living room. Through the downstairs hallway.

The tracks stopped in front of the library.

Ed turned, only Bailey was right behind him. He was close—too close. Close enough that she could feel the heat emanating from him. That she caught another whiff of his cologne. That her heart leaped into her throat.

He didn't seem affected.

He twisted the handle. "It's locked."

Bailey shook her head. "That room is never locked."

"Stay back." His tone left no room for argument.

Bailey braced herself against the wall. Her heart pounded in her ears and her breathing became labored as she waited for what would happen next.

With more skill than any DC lawyer should have, Ed kicked the door open.

Tension clenched Bailey's spine. She'd never met a suit that knew how to do that. Nor how to do it with so much confidence. As if he'd done it a million times before.

Just what kind of secrets was Ed hiding? The way he'd

handled that gun earlier had also been impressive and surprising.

He scanned the inside of the room before muttering, "Houston, we have a problem."

She gripped the iron poker even tighter. "What's wrong?"

He nodded toward the library. "Someone's been here. And they were looking for something."

She peered around the corner. The library had been demolished. Books were everywhere. Papers littered the floor. Chairs were overturned.

And that was only what she could see in the darkness. The daylight would surely reveal more injuries to the space.

She wondered who would do such a thing. Though a greater question remained.

Had the person who'd done this left or were they still lurking somewhere between the walls of this house?

THREE

Ed didn't like this. He didn't like it one bit.

Someone else had been here. They'd broken in. And they were looking for something very specific.

This had to have something to do with that phone call from his father's friend. He'd discovered something, shared that information with his father, and now they were both dead. Based on this break-in, there may have been some kind of physical intelligence exchanged. Maybe that information was still here and someone was looking for it. It was the only thing that made sense.

Had the intruder found that communication and escaped?

Or was he still here? Still looking?

Ed didn't know those answers, but somehow he had to find out.

Across the room, the window was open. A cold wind howled inside.

Most likely, whoever had been here had left out that window.

Either that, or he'd set it up to make it appear as if he'd left. In the world of espionage, things were hardly ever what they seemed.

"Ed?"

Bailey's voice pulled him out of his thoughts for a moment. "Yes?"

"What are we going to do?"

"We're going to remain cautious," he said. "That's the first thing. Stay there. Let me get this window closed."

With his gun still drawn, he crossed the room, looking for any sign of hidden, unexpected visitors. There was no one. Just as thunder filled the air, he reached the window, pulled it shut and locked it.

He returned to the door, noting Bailey was no longer lingering in the door frame where he'd left her. Had she decided to be a lone ranger? To go out on her own? Certainly the woman wasn't that neurotic.

He peered into the hallway and saw no sign of Bailey. The poker she'd been holding lay on the floor, as if she'd dropped it.

Strange. Suspicious, even.

"Bailey?" he called.

An impending feeling of malice crept into his psyche.

When there was no answer, he realized that something was wrong. Seriously wrong.

Bailey struggled against the man who'd grabbed her in the hallway.

One moment, she'd only heard Ed's voice. The next instant, thunder had cracked and a gloved hand had covered her mouth. A solid, steel-like arm had pinned her limbs against her body, making her unable to move.

She'd tried to kick and scream, but nothing. Her attacker easily overpowered her, rendering her immobile and helpless. In the blink of an eye, the man lifted her off her feet and carried her silently down the hallway.

She tried to resist, but the man was like a machine. His arms gripped her like a vise.

With amazing stealth, he carried her past the living room. Into the west wing of the house. Into the old game room with its wood paneling, stained-glass lighting and massive pool table.

He shoved her onto the leather couch. The plastic covering crinkled beneath her. Each crumple made her nerves tighten.

Every minute counted, she reminded herself. This was no time to let her fear consume her. She had to keep a clear head if she wanted to stay alive.

Her gaze jerked upward as she fought off the nausea.

The man leered at her. The black ski mask he wore made it impossible to make out any features. She saw the most important one, though. Even in the dark, she saw the hatred in his eyes.

Then she saw the knife in his hands. Five inches of shiny metal. A thick handle wrapped with what appeared to be leather. A devilishly sharp-looking blade, one that could probably slice her skin at just a whisper of a touch.

"Where is it?" the man mumbled, leaning toward her.

His voice was deep and rumbling and menacing. Her fear deepened.

He held the knife out, daring her to try to escape. He looked ready to pounce as he crouched over her. Bailey knew beyond a doubt that he'd use the knife if he had to.

She could hardly move. Hardly breathe.

All she could see was the knife. All she could think about was her life ending in pain and torture. She had so much more she wanted to do. She wanted to get married and have kids. She wanted to explore the world, to learn to knit, to make peace with the mistakes of her past.

What had he just said? He'd asked her a question. For the life of her, she couldn't remember what.

"I said, where is it?" the man said as if reading her thoughts. He held the knife closer, right at her throat. His eyes glimmered with an evil she'd never seen before.

She swallowed so hard it hurt. Swallowed so hard she

was afraid the blade might touch the delicate skin at her neck. So hard that her throat burned.

"Where is what?" She finally managed to get the words out.

Was it the stress of the situation? Was that why his question made no sense? She searched her memories, trying to figure what in the world the man was talking about. She came up with nothing.

His other hand dug into her arm. She refused to yelp, even if his fingers caused pain to jolt through her.

"Don't play stupid. The information. I need it."

The library flashed through her mind. This man had been searching for something there. Couldn't find it. He thought Bailey could, though.

What was he talking about? A will? It was the only thing that made sense at the moment. But Mr. Carter's lawyer had the will.

There was something she was missing.

Something major. She had to buy time as she figured out what.

"I don't know what you're talking about." Her voice broke under the strain of the moment. "You've got to believe me. I was just a nurse."

He paused. "You were the only one Mr. Carter spoke with in his final days. Certainly he told you something. Maybe in those delirious moments before death?"

What had he said? He'd asked Bailey to protect his things from someone who was coming. What if he hadn't been crazy? "We didn't have that kind of relationship," Bailey finally said. "Purely professional."

"You knew him better than anyone else. If anyone can find the information, it's you."

She could still feel the knife at her neck. "How can I find something if I don't know what it is?"

"You'll know when you see it. You can move freely about the house to search. I can't."

She shook her head, trying to ward away panic. Trying to figure out how to save herself. "I'm leaving tomorrow. As soon as the storm passes."

"You're not leaving until you find it," he ordered.

Her heart skipped a beat at his implications. "I think you're talking to the wrong person. I was just a nurse." How could she make him understand?

He leaned closer, his voice raspy and threatening. His breath fanned hot across her cheek, the scent of peppermint filling her nostrils. "I'm giving you one week. If you don't have the information by then, I'll kill you."

A shudder raced down her spine. "But—"

He squeezed her arm. "I'm not finished. After I kill you, I'll make sure everyone else around you pays."

"There's no one else," she muttered, desperate to keep her family safe. Their faces flashed through her mind, her heart squeezing at each sweet image. She couldn't put them in danger. She wouldn't.

"No one else, huh?" He squeezed her throat. "Do you want to rethink that?"

Panic jolted through her. He couldn't know. She just had to convince him she was all alone in the world, that there was no one to hold as leverage over her.

"There's no one else," she insisted.

He squeezed her throat harder. A small cry escaped this time. As hard as she tried to hide her fear, it seemed to be pouring out in the tears that rushed down her cheeks.

"Try again," he growled.

She stayed quiet.

"I'm tired of these games. You're the only one who can get the information I need. I repeat—you need to find it. If you don't, I'll kill your sister."

She forced herself not to show any surprise. "I'm an only child," she insisted. She hoped she sounded convincing.

"You think I'm stupid? Her name is Lauren. She lives down in Florida."

Panic made her muscles tremble. This couldn't be happening. He couldn't possibly know this.

The man squeezed again, and her airway tightened. "Got it?"

She only stared, unable to answer. The man had researched Bailey. He'd looked into her family.

This confrontation wasn't by chance. This had all been planned. Every last detail.

Except maybe Ed. There's no way someone had planned on him being here.

Right? Or was he a part of this somehow?

Nothing made sense at the moment.

Adrenaline surged through her, making her thoughts feel hypercharged.

As she stared at the man's icy gaze, she had no doubt that his threat was real. This man wouldn't blink at the thought of taking another life.

"I don't like repeating myself. Do you hear me?"

Finally, she nodded.

He leaned closer. "Don't tell anyone about our meeting. Or that I'm here. Or that we had this conversation. Got it?"

She stared again as a million scenarios played out in her mind.

"Got it?" he demanded, his voice louder, gruffer.

She nodded. "Got it."

"I have ears everywhere. Everywhere. I'll hear everything you say, so be careful. Ed Carter can't know about this. Understand?"

She nodded.

"And all of your lies just made me change my mind. If

you don't cooperate, I'll have my men *start* with your sister. Then her kids. Alex and Emma."

Bailey sucked in a deep breath at the mention of their names.

Then he raised his knife. Something hard hit her head and she passed out.

Ed checked all the rooms on the lower wing, where his dad's office was located. He didn't find Bailey anywhere.

He searched for footprints. For signs of a struggle. For anything that would give an indication of what had happened to the woman.

He'd found nothing.

He paused in the living room, trying to figure out his next plan of action. The footprints left earlier at the door hadn't been disturbed.

He had a few options left. The west wing. Upstairs. The widow's walk. Or the back of the house, where the kitchen, dining room and pantry were located.

He paused for a moment and listened for any telltale sounds. Silence answered him.

Until the wood floor creaked in the distance.

He spun and saw Bailey standing at the entrance of the west wing, a dazed expression on her face. She rubbed her head with one hand. The other arm was flung across her chest in an almost protective gesture. Her hair looked disheveled, and he thought he saw a tremble claiming all of her muscles.

"Are you okay?" He crossed the room in long strides to meet her, to begin to assess what had happened.

She nodded, a new emotion in her gaze. She almost seemed dazed. Ed had seen the stunned expression in an instant, but the next moment it disappeared. She'd blinked and her walls had gone up. Her jaw hardened and she sucked in a long, deep breath.

"Of course I'm fine. Why?"

He stared at her, dumbfounded. How could she act so calm? Just what had happened? Something was off. "You're fine?"

She shrugged and raised her chin. "Why wouldn't I be?"

Ed didn't miss the way her throat tightened, almost as if she was having trouble swallowing because of the tension welling inside her.

"Why wouldn't you be fine? How about because one minute you were in the library and the next moment you were gone." There was something she wasn't telling him and that realization left him unsettled.

She shrugged again. "I just decided to check things out for myself."

A smattering of rain against the window sent her clinging to the wall, her gaze swinging wildly about. She could talk tough all she wanted, but her actions told the truth.

"*You* decided to check things out yourself? You? The woman who walked so closely behind me that I could barely move? You suddenly got enough courage to explore this dark house on your own?" Something wasn't adding up, and he didn't like where all of this was going.

"I'm not as spineless as you might think I am." She raised her chin even higher.

He still saw the tremble racing through her.

"What aren't you saying, Bailey?" He stepped closer so he could see the truth in her eyes.

Something flashed there again. Fear? Defiance?

He wasn't sure.

"We're not in this together, you know," she finally muttered. "I was doing just fine here before you showed up."

He stepped closer. "Were you? If I hadn't shown up and you'd run into some stranger who'd broken into the house with less than honorable intentions, I'd doubt you'd act so laid-back."

"I've always done things on my own. I just decided to take matters into my own hands and see if the intruder was still here. We were wasting time sticking together."

He didn't buy her story for a second. "And was he?"

She swallowed so hard that her throat muscles visibly tightened. "You didn't see him. Did you?"

He shifted, his hands going to his hips. He reminded himself that Bailey, most likely, wasn't one of the bad guys here. He didn't need to go into interrogation mode. "You need to tell me what kind of game you're playing. Otherwise, we might both end up dead."

Wrinkles appeared at the corner of her eyes. "Look, I'm sorry. I won't wander away again. I had a moment of bad judgment."

That little excuse wasn't going to settle with him. But she wasn't saying anything else right now.

He'd keep an eye on her. He didn't trust her.

But for now, they had to work together.

He couldn't be 100 percent sure that the intruder was gone. Whoever it had been had definitely set it up to look as if he'd left. But the person behind this vandalism wasn't a newbie. They were experienced...and possibly working with Bailey?

He had to keep that idea at the forefront of his mind.

Trust no one.

That had been his mantra for more than a decade.

He didn't see it changing anytime soon.

FOUR

Bailey rubbed her throat, suddenly exhausted, weary and overwhelmed. "What now?"

"Right now we secure the house and batten down the hatches, so to speak, for this storm. Until it's daylight, there's not much more we can do except try to stay safe and keep our eyes open."

Bailey nodded. As she felt Ed's gaze on her, she rubbed her throat again. He wasn't stupid. He knew she wasn't telling the truth. But she had no other choice at this point. She had to do whatever she had to to keep her family safe. She needed time to think, to figure things out. Her adrenaline wanted to race ahead as her mind struggled through the possibilities.

"I know where all of the entrances to the house are," Bailey offered. "I can show you and we can make sure they're secure."

Ed nodded. "Good idea. We'll stick together."

She wouldn't argue with that. She had no desire to wander this place by herself. "Let's go."

They moved throughout the house, checking windows and doors. They said very little as they worked. Bailey tried to ignore the tension between them, tried to pretend that everything was like it was before. Everything hadn't been great earlier, but now her conscience bothered her. Now she *did* have a secret and, along with it, she had guilt.

Just two hours ago, things had seemed relatively simple. She'd planned on reading her novel, turning in for the night, and in the morning she'd depart this place and look for a new job. Though she'd been dreading starting over again, right now she dreaded staying here even more. Especially under these circumstances.

How could two hours turn her life upside down?

Finally, Ed checked the last window. It was latched.

"We're secure," he said.

But Bailey knew that nothing was really secure. Someone very likely was still in this house with them. Where? She had no idea. She hadn't seen a sign of him as they'd moved throughout the place. Whoever this man was, he was good. He had the ability to disappear. Maybe he'd even planted cameras somewhere. That fact had her on edge.

"Let's get back to that fire," Ed suggested. "It's freezing in here."

Finally, they went down to the living room. Bailey knelt in front of the flames, absorbing the heat for a moment. She only wished the flames could warm her heart as it did her hands. Despair and panic did a tangled dance inside her.

Ed's voice broke through her thoughts. "Any food left here?"

"I donated most of it and threw away the perishables." She shrugged. "I was planning on leaving in the morning and I didn't want it to be wasted."

Except, she couldn't now. She had to think of some way to stay. That meant that she should probably get on Ed's good side, especially since this was his place now.

"I did save some crackers, cheese, peanut butter and a few apples to snack on until I left. I think there's coffee and some of that fancy tea your dad liked, also. Would you like me to get them for you?"

He stared again. The man obviously didn't trust her. He shouldn't trust her, at this point. Bailey had always been the kind of person people could depend on, the one people told their secrets to. She didn't even know how to be untrustworthy, which only added to this crisis of conscience.

"I'll get the food," Ed finally said. "Where did you leave everything?"

"The kitchen counter. Beside the refrigerator. In a basket." She'd been planning on taking it with her on the boat. Then she'd call a taxi from the piers to take her to the rental-car agency. She'd been planning on going down to see her sister.

Ed stepped away. Being away from him both made her relax and feel tenser at the same time. She was glad to be away from his scrutiny, but she couldn't help worry as she sat alone in the dark.

Her thoughts revolved around Ed and his credibility. Why hadn't Mr. Carter kept any pictures of his son around the house? What kind of relationship had the two of them had? Mr. Carter had certainly spoken with pride about his only offspring, but if they had such a close relationship, why hadn't Ed shown up for his father's last days? Something wasn't adding up. A lot of things, for that matter. What if Ed wasn't who he'd claimed to be?

She shrugged it off and grabbed some blankets from the closet, leaving a few on the couch in case Ed needed them. Then she pulled the leather recliner closer to the fireplace and settled there, pulling several blankets over herself. The temperature had dropped, and the air in the house was more than chilly. It was downright uncomfortable.

As another shiver washed over her, she looked over her shoulder. Was the stranger watching her now? Was he waiting for just the right moment to flaunt his power over her? Nausea turned in her stomach at the thoughts.

Ed appeared with a tray a few minutes later. He'd scrounged up not only some crackers and apples but also a few bottles of water. He set them on the table between them. "I thought you might be hungry, as well."

She swallowed hard. "Thank you."

As soon as the words left her mouth, her stomach grumbled. It seemed she was hungrier than she'd thought. She leaned forward and grabbed some crackers. If anything, they might help to settle her stomach, which was twisted in knots.

Ed sat on the couch, ignoring the blankets in favor of leaning closer to the fire, and grabbed an apple. "How long did you work for my father, Bailey?"

Bailey ran a finger over her lips, hoping to dislodge any stray crumbs. "Eight months."

"And how'd you end up on an isolated place like Smuggler's Cove?"

She shrugged, thinking back on the broken path that had led to her decision to come here. "Long story. I needed some changes in my life. I had worked as a nurse in the ER, but I was tired of the pace, the pressure, the social scene of life back in Raleigh. I decided maybe I should be a home health nurse and applied with an agency. A day later, I got the call about your father."

"I'm surprised you lasted more than a week around that ornery man." He offered a wry smile.

The mystery of their relationship deepened. The way Ed said the words was with an unmistakable affection, but that didn't add up with the facts she already knew. "Your father was a wonderful man. I mean, he was kind of gruff sometimes. But once you got past those walls, he was delightful. I loved listening to his stories."

He took another bite of his apple and leaned back. "What kind of stories?"

"Of traveling the world. Of the people he met. Of how our country has changed since he was a boy. He took a lot of pride in the United States and the freedoms we have here."

"My dad told you all of that?"

She nodded. "We had nothing to do but talk. I mean, sometimes we took walks outside or sat by the water or I read books to him. But mostly we talked."

Ed's face tightened, and Bailey wondered about his expression. What was he thinking? That she was lying and that his father couldn't possibly be that kind? Or did he regret that he'd missed out on his father's final days?

"Did he talk about his work very much?"

Bailey shrugged. "I don't know. He did mention some of the senators he had to work with and some of the places he got to visit. He usually only talked about that if he had company."

Ed raised his eyebrows. "Company?"

Bailey nodded. "He had some people from work visit him a few times." *At least someone had cared enough to.* She kept that thought silent.

Ed tilted his head to the side. "I thought my father wanted to get away from everything—and everyone. Especially work. He associated it with too much pressure, pressure he didn't need with his heart condition."

Maybe that's what Ed told himself to justify not coming to visit himself. Speaking of which...

She stared at Ed a moment, wondering what kind of heartless man didn't visit his dad in his final days. Whether she liked it or not, it appeared she'd be finding out.

Ed saw the judgment in Bailey's eyes. He wanted to pretend that he didn't care, but he knew he did. He didn't have to explain himself to Bailey, though. God was the only one who needed to understand, and the two of them had already had many talks about everything that had gone down.

Claire had judged him enough that he'd had his fill. The two had dated for a year and Ed had hoped to marry her one day. She was an executive assistant for a company in DC and had to travel a couple of weekends a month for work.

At least, that was her cover story.

In reality, she was working for an elite group of international spies determined to steal US secrets. Ed—and dating Ed—had been a part of the plan she'd devised to get information from him. Thankfully, Ed had seen the light, so to speak, in the nick of time. He'd been heartbroken and angry. Then he'd simply poured more of himself into his work.

"Why are you here, Ed? Why did you come now and not earlier?"

Bailey's voice pulled him out of his thoughts. He turned toward the woman, ignoring the strange desire he had to trust her. Trust made people weak, and he couldn't afford that right now. What he'd said earlier was true. Bailey had the most access to his father. She, for all intents and purposes, should be his first suspect.

"I'm here because someone murdered my father, and I intend to find out who."

Any enemies would have been wise to hire someone with an innocent face like Bailey. She seemed so unsuspecting, and that would make her the perfect culprit. There was a part of him that wanted to believe there were good people in the world, but experience told him to remain cautious.

"I really don't understand. Why would you think he was murdered?" She finished her cracker, leaned back in the chair and pulled her blanket to her chin.

He shrugged. "I have my reasons. Did anything out of the ordinary happen in the days leading up to his death?"

She drew in a deep breath and looked off into the distance a moment. "He did ask me to protect his things. He said something about someone coming here and destroying people. We'd just watched an action movie on TV, though. I thought maybe he was confusing TV with real life."

Interesting. He'd continue to let her think his father's words had been accidental. But Ed knew the truth.

Nothing was as it seemed, and Ed didn't know who to trust—including his colleagues at the CIA. He couldn't help but wonder if they were involved somehow. Was all of this a cover-up on their part?

"I can't imagine why anyone would want to kill your dad," Bailey whispered. "He said he was just a number cruncher at the State Department. Certainly that's no reason that he'd be in danger—unless adding something up incorrectly is reason for murder."

"Sounds like you've been watching too many spy movies."

She frowned. "Yeah, maybe I have. But I'm not the one who thinks Mr. Carter was murdered."

He bit down, knowing he couldn't say anything and fluctuating between being amused and irritated. "Maybe you should get some rest. It's been a long night."

Bailey frowned and pulled the covers up around her shoulders.

Ed wouldn't be getting any rest, not knowing the fact that someone else had been in this house. Until he knew what was going on, he'd be on the lookout.

Morning sunlight streamed through the windows as Bailey opened her eyes. It seemed against all odds she'd fallen asleep. The last thing she remembered was staring at the fire, trying to figure out the craziness that had become her life. She'd been determined to stay awake, to keep a lookout for danger. So much for that plan.

She blinked a couple of times before everything came

into focus. Ed squatted by the fire, adding more logs to the flames. He looked up when he noticed her stirring.

"Morning," he mumbled.

She pushed herself up in the recliner. "Morning."

Thoughts of yesterday continued to swirl in her head. The man. The threat. Lauren. Ed. Mr. Carter.

She nearly groaned. She'd so desperately wanted all of this to simply be a nightmare. Reality felt like a cold slap in the face.

She needed to think of a way to convince Ed to let her stay. She needed to look for that information. She'd wasted time already. She should have started looking last night, but she knew that she was under Ed's watchful eye and she was no good at being sneaky.

"I'm not sure when the ferry will start running again," she began. "But I was thinking about sticking around for a little bit longer, until things settle down a bit."

"I'm nearly certain transportation to the mainland will be back up today. Half of the island evacuated, and I'm sure residents will be interested in getting back to check out the damage."

"Yes, and a lot of them may need help," Bailey countered, desperate to sound natural, despite the anxiety racing through her. "I'd hate to leave everyone in their time of need."

"That's kind of you, but don't feel obligated. I know you need to look for another job."

"As a matter of fact, your father arranged to have me paid for a few weeks after his death. That was just one more reason I stuck around to help tie up loose ends. I almost feel indebted to stay here and earn my keep." Her heart pounded. The excuse sounded believable to her. Would Ed go for it?

Ed stood. "Sounds like my father. He liked to take care of people."

Bailey shrugged, not ready to give up quite yet on convincing Ed. "Well, the people on the island have become like family. You should be there for family when they need you."

Ed did the stare. The look was becoming all too familiar.

Bailey grabbed an apple from the table and stood up, stretching. She immediately missed her blankets. She had to push aside any sign of weakness, though, and prove herself to Ed.

She needed to somehow earn his trust while keeping him at arm's length. There were still so many uncertainties about him; he was hiding something.

"I almost dread seeing the damage outside. Mr. Wilkins, the groundskeeper, evacuated before the storm," Bailey said. "I'm not sure when he'll be back."

Bailey strode over to the front door and pulled it open. She was expecting to survey the landscape outside. Instead, she stifled a scream at the towering figure standing there.

FIVE

"I reckon since the power's out, the doorbell's not working. I've been standing here for five minutes. I've got a delivery for Ed Carter."

Bailey nearly laughed at herself. The figure wasn't quite as towering as she'd thought.

Alvin stood there. He was the town's "chauffeur," which really meant that he ran people around in his golf cart. He had two suitcases at his feet and, based on his tapping foot, he was in a hurry.

Ed stepped up behind Bailey. "Thanks, Alvin. I appreciate you bringing those by."

"No problem."

Ed reached into his wallet, pulled out some bills and slapped them into Alvin's hands. "How's the water level? Is the island still flooded?" Ed asked.

"It's down right now, but only because it's low tide," Alvin said. "Come high tide, the bridge leading to your property is going to be covered again. That was one nasty storm. There's no electricity on the island right now, and I can't remember the last time that happened."

"Let us know if anyone needs anything," Ed offered, sounding halfway human for a change.

"Much obliged. Thank you." Alvin tipped his hat and hurried back to his golf cart.

Bailey enjoyed hearing the accents of the locals. The island was once known to be a hiding spot for pirates. After the place was settled, the people who lived here had been so far removed from other civilization that the accent of the original English settlers had stuck around for decades. Only in recent years had it begun to fade as TVs became more popular and travel between the island and the mainland became easier.

Ed grabbed his luggage and set the suitcases inside the door. As he moved out of the way, Bailey got her first real glimpse of the outside in the morning sunlight.

The landscape looked as if a tornado had gone through. Tree limbs and leaves were everywhere. Part of someone's roof was strewn in the distance, as well as some pickets and a trash can.

On the shore, mounds of seaweed and other "treasures" from the bay that often got washed onto the sand with storms were visible. No doubt there were sand dollars and horseshoe crabs and shells. There would also be litter— shoes, fishing line, pieces of damaged boats and piers.

It was going to take a lot of cleaning up to get this place back in order.

Now she just had to convince Ed that he needed her help to do so and that it was going to take more than an extra day or two.

"We've got a big job ahead of us this week," she told him.

"We?" He raised an eyebrow.

She crossed her arms. "You need help. Admit it. You can't clean all of this up on your own. You're going to need to hire someone to help. It might as well be me. All I charge is room and board."

He stared at her, that same incredulous expression on his face. "You want to help? After everything that happened last night? Even knowing that I still suspect you could have something to do with my father's death?"

"I've already told you that I loved your father like he was my own. I'd never hurt him. And, yes, I really do want to help. I'm not one to leave things unfinished."

Finally, he shrugged. "Well, I won't turn it down. I will need help. At least for today."

He walked over toward the fire and picked up a mug, taking a long sip.

Bailey leaned closer. "What are you drinking?"

The electricity was out, but it almost smelled like...

"Coffee. Why?" He took another sip.

She stepped closer, trying not to salivate. "How did you make that?"

"I've learned a few tricks while camping over the years. I made it over the fireplace." He pulled the mug back, his eyes sparkling. "Would you like some?"

"All I charge is room and board—and coffee. I'm revising my earlier statement."

"That's good, because I wasn't going to pay you anyway." A hint of a smile tugged at his lips.

He poured her a cup of caffeinated bliss. The man could go from irritating her to charming her in 5.2 seconds. But when he placed the mug in her hands, gratefulness was all she felt. She took a long sip, hoping the caffeine would give her the boost she needed to get through the day. She'd hardly slept at all last night, and she felt it now.

She took another sip of her coffee. She had to figure out a way to find the "information" the man had mentioned. Did Ed know what it was? Even if he did, it wasn't likely he would tell her. She needed a plan, and she needed it now.

Ed grabbed his suitcase and took a step toward the stairway. "I'm going to get changed. Meet me outside in twenty?"

"I thought I might start in the library since it's such a mess from last night. Is that okay?"

He stared at her a moment. "Good idea. I'll help you. We'll work together."

She nodded stiffly. He didn't trust her, either.

The fact remained that she'd need a lot more ideas than helping with the cleanup if she wanted to stay long enough to find answers, though.

Right now, she had to figure out how to buy herself more time.

As much as Ed didn't want to admit it, Bailey was a good worker. She didn't complain as they straightened up the library, replaced books, tidied papers and cleaned up broken picture frames. Even when a piece of glass had cut her hand, she'd simply wrapped it in a paper towel, donned some gloves and continued working.

As he watched her now—her expression innocent and determined—he had a hard time continuing to think of her as a suspect. Somehow, he had to get some details out of her. He needed to know who'd been here in the weeks before his father died, if he'd talked to anyone unusual on the phone, if he'd said anything out of character in his final moments.

Ed had to get to the bottom of this, not only for the company's sake, but for his own personal peace of mind. He'd made Bailey practically beg to stay here, but secretly he needed her here until he could figure out her role in all of this. But if she turned out to be innocent, he needed to get her off this island and away from danger. He didn't want any more casualties. The fact that his dad and his dad's friend had died was two too many.

While they'd cleaned, he'd looked for anything suspicious, anything that would offer answers on his father's death. He'd found nothing.

Whoever was lurking on the property didn't want to

be discovered and had enough knowledge to conceal any evidence.

That meant that, just as he'd suspected when he'd first seen his dad's ransacked library, the intruder was most likely a professional. He'd come here for a specific purpose, and he wouldn't stop until he had what he wanted. The realization caused his stomach to tightened.

He stood and stretched for a moment. "I'm going to work outside for a while. Why don't you join me when you're done?"

Bailey nodded. "No problem."

He really just wanted to look for footprints or any other clues. Not that he expected to find any. He'd spent most of the night trying to come up with a plan of action. He'd narrowed down his agenda. He'd get to know Bailey, find out what she knew. He also needed to get to know the people in town, ascertain whether or not they'd seen anything suspicious. While maintaining his own low profile.

As a cool October wind swept over the yard, he stopped and sucked in a deep breath. It felt good to simply take a moment to pause. For so long, he'd simply been living for his job. He'd nearly forgotten who he was in the process. He'd forgotten how he liked to work with his hands, go boating, smell the ocean breeze.

But the break was over all too soon. He checked around the windows for footprints. There was nothing, but that wasn't a surprise. He began nailing a shingle back onto the side of the house when he spotted Bailey walking his way.

"I just finished up in the library." She pointed to the plastic billowing from the broken window a few feet away. "I think there's some plywood in the garage. Do you want to cover the window that broke? I'm sure we won't be able to get a new one for a while. In a house this old it will probably have to be special ordered."

He nodded. "Good idea."

He grabbed his tools, took one more glance at his hand-iwork and felt satisfied. As they walked side by side, the breeze carried with it the scent of daisies. Since there were no flowers anywhere to be seen, he could only conclude that despite their primitive conditions, Bailey still managed to smell like a field of wildflowers.

He could get used to that scent.

As he glanced over, the wind lifted Bailey's hair a moment. What he saw made him pause.

He grasped Bailey's arm and pulled her to a stop. "Is that a bruise?"

Concern filled her gaze as her hand went to her neck. She knew exactly what he was talking about.

Still, she mumbled, "No. No bruise."

She tried to keep walking, but Ed pulled her to a stop again. "There's something on your neck."

She shrugged, emotions flashing in her eyes. Fear. The woman was scared, wasn't she? But why?

"I'm fine. Probably from a book that fell on me when I reached too high on the shelf to return it."

He raised his eyebrows. "That's your story?"

The woman was a horrible liar. Ed considered that a good attribute, refreshing.

She raised her chin, avoiding his gaze. "Whether you believe me or not, it's really not your concern."

He wanted to say more. To say so much more. But it wasn't his place.

All he could think was that it looked as though someone had grabbed her by the throat. Threatened her maybe? The injury looked fresh, as if it had just happened recently.

The unsettled feeling continued to churn in his gut.

For the rest of the morning and into the afternoon, Bailey tugged at her shirt, trying to cover the tender area around her neck, evidence of the threat she'd gotten last night. Evidence of the turmoil she was feeling.

Ed's attention to her bruises had been the last thing she'd wanted. She couldn't afford for him to ask too many questions. The man in the ski mask had said if she told anyone, he'd kill her sister. She would never, ever let that happen. She couldn't risk her sister's safety, no matter how desperate she felt at the moment. As Ed repaired the back door from where he'd kicked it in, she tasked herself with raking some of the colorful leaves from the live oak trees.

It wasn't what she wanted to be doing. She wanted to find the information her attacker wanted and get off this island. But she had to plan each of her moves carefully. Bide her time. She needed to earn a bit of Ed's trust.

In the distance, she heard Ed's cell phone ring. As she glanced at him, he stopped hammering and stepped away to take the call.

Bailey's throat burned as she watched him. Though the man was a lawyer, he certainly looked good with a hammer. Earlier, he'd changed into jeans and a long-sleeved black T-shirt. The beginning of a beard covered his cheeks and chin.

He caught her staring as he hung up and walked back her way. His shoulders didn't seem quite so heavy. Still, she realized there was something he wasn't telling her. The mystery around him continued to grow deeper.

Just then, her cell phone buzzed. She glanced down at the text on her screen.

Don't work too hard and forget your task.

The blood drained from her face and she glanced around. The man who'd threatened her was watching her now. But where? Was there anywhere she was away from his listening ears or watchful eye?

"That was my father's lawyer," Ed announced. "The will is being read on Friday in Richmond. He was making sure I could be there."

Bailey flinched as Ed's voice brought her back to the present. She quickly slipped her phone back into her pocket. "What?"

He stared at her, curiosity in his gaze. "I said, my father's will is being read on Friday."

Bailey couldn't help but wonder if that inheritance was the only reason Ed had come back.

"He wants you there, too."

Surprise flashed through her. "Me?"

"That's right."

"I couldn't possibly take anything from your father."

Ed shrugged, still distant, cool. "He obviously felt different."

An idea hit her. This might be the answer she was looking for. "Okay. Well, then, I might as well stick around until then rather than go down to Florida to be with my sister, only to come back up."

Ed opened his mouth to say something when someone walking up the lane caught both their eyes. Relief washed through Bailey when she spotted a familiar blonde.

"Samantha!" Bailey abandoned the leaves and went to join her friend.

"I wanted to come check on you," Samantha said, pulling her into a hug. "That was a rough storm. How's it going?"

"We survived. The yard barely did, though. It's still a mess."

Samantha glanced behind her, her eyes glinting with curiosity. "We?"

"Of course." Bailey felt her cheeks flush as she turned toward Ed. "Samantha, this is Ed Carter, Bill's son."

Samantha smiled and extended her hand. "So nice to meet you."

Ed smiled politely. Maybe he had manners around everyone except Bailey. "Nice to meet you, too."

"Samantha lives on the other side of the island," Bailey continued. "Her fiancé just restored some old fishing cabins there."

"Bailey and I both showed up here in Smuggler's Cove about the same time and instantly bonded," Samantha added. "So besides coming to see how you fared after last night, I was wondering if you wanted to come by for a cookout tonight. We have a freezer full of fish at our place and if we don't get our electricity back, all of those fillets are going to go bad." She glanced at Ed. "You, too."

"That would be great," Bailey said. She would love to spend more time with Samantha. Maybe getting away from this house for an hour or two would do her good. She hadn't found anything in the library. She'd quickly searched Mr. Carter's bedroom as well, but there was nothing. Those were the two rooms he'd used most. She hardly knew where to look next.

"Ed?" Samantha asked.

He shook his head. "Thanks for the invitation, but I probably shouldn't."

"Okay, but I can't imagine you have much food left here. I know Bailey donated a bunch to the church. That was just yesterday, wasn't it?"

Bailey nodded. At least Samantha backed up the fact that Bailey was telling the truth. Ed now had proof that Bailey truly *was* planning to leave. She hadn't simply been freeloading on his father's property.

Finally Ed nodded, although a bit hesitantly. "Sure, dinner sounds good. I don't want to impose, though."

"If you're a friend of Bailey's, then you're a friend of mine," Samantha said. "We'd love to have you."

Bailey wasn't exactly sure she'd call Ed a friend. But a strange relief did fill her. Maybe Ed would finally let down his guard tonight and reveal something about himself.

If Samantha got to the bottom of who he really was, the answers might help her locate the elusive information, as well.

SIX

"I haven't ridden a bicycle in years." Ed gripped the handlebars and cruised down the path leading from his father's house. The sun hit his shoulders, reminding him of the time he'd spent down in Laos. The beaches had been beautiful, and bikes were common transportation. He'd been there on one of his first assignments. Back when he'd been idealistic and headstrong. Over the years, he'd become jaded and skeptical.

Bailey grinned beside him as her hair billowed behind her. Being out of that house seemed to help her relax considerably. Some of the strain left her features, replaced with an image of an all-American girl—woman, he should say. She just seemed so wholesome and natural out here.

"Biking is my favorite way to get around the island," she said.

He veered to the right to avoid a root in his path. "I never could understand why my dad would want to come somewhere with no cars and no easy access to the mainland."

"It helps you to slow down," Bailey said. "The slower pace is actually kind of nice. I know I've grown accustomed to it. I'm not sure how I'm going to handle getting back into the rat race. Being here made me feel like a kid again. We'd take family vacations to the beach growing up, and I loved riding my bike on the boardwalk. We'd stay at this beach house with an overlook at the top. I'd sneak up there as much as I could so I could read my books."

"Sounds nice."

Her grin slipped. "It was. My mom and dad have both passed away since then. My mom died of cancer, my dad of a heart attack. Those family vacations…well, they seem like another lifetime ago."

"I can understand that," Ed offered.

Silence fell between them for a few minutes.

"So, what did you do for fun around here?" Ed finally asked. "When you weren't working?"

"I was on call nearly all the time," Bailey said, gliding over the sandy path. "But, when I could, I would enjoy the beach for a while. I especially liked looking for dolphins at sunset. Sometimes I read up on the widow's walk. There's a great little ice cream place in town, and Erma's restaurant has scrumptious crab soup." She shrugged. "Mostly, I just liked letting my mind feel uncluttered."

What would that be like? What would it feel like to be able to relax, to not always look over your shoulder, to actually trust someone for once? He couldn't even imagine.

"Tell me about your friend. Samantha, right?" Ed wished he was asking for friendly reasons. But his life boiled down to the fact that he had to be suspicious of everyone, especially the ones who seemed the most innocent.

"She's great. I met her and her fiancé at church. Samantha has the cutest little boy. He's around eight years old. Maybe nine by now? Her fiancé is John Wagner, and he's a former Coastie."

A Coastie? Maybe this dinner wouldn't be a waste of his time. As much as he wanted to dig into the death of his father, he was going to have to gather more information first. Getting to know a few of the locals could work to his advantage—not that he only wanted to view people for what they could do for him. Of course, in his line of work, that was too often the case.

Which was one more reason maybe it was time for him to consider a career change.

"Turn right here," Bailey directed him.

She veered her bike onto a path through the woods. The ground was soggy from last night's storm. On a good day, small bridges connected various parts of the island. Today, they'd had to ride through several areas where the water nearly reached their bike pedals.

The nice part about riding through town was seeing everyone out in their yards, pitching in to help each other. Maybe that was another reason why his dad had liked this place so much. It was like stepping back in time. It was too bad that his father hadn't been able to enjoy it longer than he had, though. His heart problems had limited what he could and couldn't do.

The skin on Ed's neck suddenly bristled. He slowed his pace and glanced through the grove of live oak trees that surrounded them on either side of the trail.

Someone was out there. They were watching Ed and Bailey. He could feel it.

"What's wrong?" Bailey asked.

Ed didn't say anything. He didn't want to alarm her, especially not until he knew more details.

He continued to scan the woods for a sign of someone. He saw nothing.

But that gut intuition told him there were eyes on them, that someone was watching.

Maybe the same person who'd killed his father?

"Ed, you're scaring me. What's going on?" Bailey asked. She slowed her pace.

Just then, the horizon cleared and the beach came into view. He tried to put aside his worries. "I thought I heard something. Probably just a bird," he insisted.

Everything in him wanted to go back and search that grove of trees. He knew it was no use, though. Whoever was there would be long gone by the time he searched every crevice.

The person watching hadn't tried to harm them. But someone was studying them. Maybe waiting for the right time to strike? Trying to figure out their routines, their patterns?

Ahead, nine cabins came into view. They were each white and neat; the perfect place for a getaway or a fishing weekend. A nice place to unplug and relax, Ed thought.

The smell of charcoal billowed toward them with the breeze. In the distance, a boy ran down the shoreline with a red merle Australian shepherd by his side. It seemed like the idyllic picture of the American dream.

They parked their bikes on a flat stretch of sandy dune grass and Bailey directed him to follow her toward a couple standing at the grill. Based on the way the two smiled at each other, they were incredibly happy and in love.

He wished that was even a possibility for his future. He didn't know if he could ever trust someone enough to seriously date again, nonetheless to ever get married. He'd been trained not to trust people, and the one time he'd let down his guard, he'd been wrong to do so.

"Bailey! So glad you made it," Samantha called, draping a dish towel over her shoulder. "You, too, Ed."

The man at the grill lowered the lid, put down his spatula and extended his hand. "John Wagner."

"Ed Carter. Thanks for having us." Ed quickly assessed the man as they shook hands. John was tall with thick, dark hair and a quiet, strong demeanor. His eyes were perceptive, but seemed steady and trustworthy.

"This is the nice thing about small-town living," John said. "Everyone can look out for each other. You certainly don't get that in some of your larger metropolitan areas. At least, not in my experience."

As the two women went inside, chatting away, Ed leaned against the picnic table. "I can't argue with that."

"Where are you from?" John asked, flipping a flaky white fish fillet.

"I'm an attorney in the DC area."

"Sounds interesting. I'm sorry to hear about your dad. I only met him once. He and Bailey were getting ice cream at the parlor in town. He seemed like a nice man."

"He softened up a lot in his older years."

John nodded. "People have a tendency to do that. He was all the talk of the town. That house of his is impressive, to say the least. Everyone always thought he was very mysterious. Speaking of mysterious, I've noticed a lot of boats around your pier lately. Hope you don't mind me saying so. As a Coastie, I'm always watching the water."

"Thanks for letting me know. I want to know what's going on around the property. There are unscrupulous people out there. Have you seen the boats often?"

John shrugged. "Several times. Two boats mainly. I'm not sure if the people on board are just fascinated with your dad's house or what. But they seem to linger. Caught them having a picnic on shore once, also."

Ed stored the facts away. They could just be innocent boaters. Or they could have other motivations.

They made chitchat for a few more minutes until the fish were done. Bailey and Samantha brought out some potato salad, cucumbers and rolls, and they all settled down to eat.

A young boy sat down with them, his dog sitting at his feet.

"Ed, this is Connor and his dog, Rusty," Samantha said.

He gave the dog a pat on the head. "Nice to meet you both."

Connor eyed him warily. "You, too."

The conversation took off from there, filled with quips from Connor about kickball tournaments, and knickknacks he'd found on the shore after the storm, and how great Rusty was at catching Frisbees.

Every once in a while, Ed couldn't help but pause and look around to make sure no one was watching them. He couldn't let down his guard, not even for a moment. Not until he knew what was going on. The only reason his father would have been killed was if he knew something he shouldn't.

The dinner felt way too normal for Ed. Here, there were no politics. No one wanted anything. It was a wholesome picnic. The fact that it wasn't strange felt *strange*.

"So, Bailey, when are you going back?" John asked. "I know the storm delayed you."

Bailey cringed. The action was so subtle that Ed had almost missed it. What was it about the question that made her uncomfortable? Why did she want to stay so badly? Was it the will? Was she after his father's money? Or was her agenda even darker, deadly even?

"I'm going to stick around a few more days. Help with the cleanup efforts."

Ed squinted. He needed to push her a little, see if he could figure her out.

"I think I can manage okay," Ed said, carefully measuring his words so he could see her reaction. "There's really not much to do."

"It's a lot for one person, though," Bailey insisted.

"I think I can handle it. I know you're probably anxious to get on with your life. Now that I think about it, you don't have to be there to meet with the lawyer. I could get him to send you a certified letter. It might make things easier."

Bailey turned toward Samantha and frowned. "Apparently, I'm named in Mr. Carter's will."

"Really? And you had no idea?" Samantha asked.

Bailey shook her head. "No clue. I mean, I don't expect anything. That's not why I do this job."

Her words sounded sincere, but were they? Ed had seen her lie and he'd seen her tell the truth. Based on those observations, her words right now were honest. Still, there was something she was hiding.

"You going to sell the place after you get it cleaned up from the storm?" John turned to Ed and asked.

The subject changed, and he still didn't have a straight answer from Bailey. He was going to continue bringing up her insistence on staying, though. He needed answers.

And so did John. He looked on expectantly as Ed figured out how to respond. He hadn't given much thought about what to do with his dad's home until John asked, but he'd never envisioned himself staying on in a place like Smuggler's Cove. He'd thought of himself as more of a DC kind of guy. After all, he had no reason to keep a house that big on an island this secluded.

Something stopped him from saying that, though. Instead, he shrugged. "I haven't decided yet."

Bailey stared at him, an unreadable expression in her eyes.

"Really?" she finally said. She took another bite of her fish, followed by a long sip of the tea from a mason jar.

He nodded slowly. "I like to take my time with decisions like these."

"Admit it—even though you came at a bad time, you're falling in love with Smuggler's Cove," Samantha added with a grin. She pushed the platter of grilled fish his way. "It happens to the best of us."

"You plan on staying here long?" John asked.

He helped himself to another piece of flounder, pondering the question. He had his leave time and staying seemed like the most logical idea. It hadn't an hour ago, but now he felt undeniably sure. "Yeah, I will be here awhile. I've got to get my father's affairs in order. Maybe I can take a load off in the process."

The conversation around Bailey faded from her consciousness as her pressing thoughts invaded every part of her mind.

Bailey had to come up with another plan. The thing was that she hated plans. In fact, she had no idea what she'd do when she left here. One of the things she'd enjoyed about being a nurse here was the fact that each day was different and filled with new possibilities. She'd been accused on more than one occasion of being a free spirit.

She'd hoped that Ed wouldn't ask any more questions. She knew he was suspicious of her excuses for staying. Her reason had seemed believable. There had been a huge storm here. Whether Ed admitted it or not, he could use a hand. And with the will being read…

Maybe she was reading too much into things. Maybe he wasn't trying to get rid of her. But what if he was? What if he had some kind of gut indicator that told him she had ulterior motives?

Bailey tried to concentrate on the conversation around her. Ed and John seemed to hit it off, talking about government work and fishing spots. Samantha, at the moment, was occupied with Connor.

"What do you say, Bailey?" Samantha asked.

Bailey looked up and saw everyone staring at her. She wiped her mouth with a cheerful paper napkin, hoping to buy some time. Her gaze focused on the Samantha, the one who'd asked the question. "What was that?"

Samantha smiled. "I said if you stuck around for a while, maybe we could all go out on the boat sometime. If we have nice weather, that is."

"That sounds nice." She was going to miss her friend when she eventually left Smuggler's Cove.

As the sun started to set, and after a sufficient amount of coffee and leftover apple pie had been consumed, Bailey's eyes met Ed's. "I guess we should get going, huh?" she offered.

"Probably a good idea."

They thanked Samantha and John before hopping on their bikes and starting back to the huge mansion that had been Bailey's home for almost a year. The sharp breeze that had risen made it hard to talk, and maybe that was a good thing.

Except that as they were putting up their bikes, Ed turned to her. She couldn't deny or pretend to ignore that he wanted to talk to her.

"Why do you want to stay so badly?" he asked.

What did she tell him? None of her excuses seemed real enough.

So she decided to go with the truth. "Because I want to know if something happened to your father just as much as you do."

Maybe more.

Because if she didn't find out, the lives of her family would be on the line.

He nodded, seeming to accept her answer. "Listen, you're welcome to stay if you'd like, maybe until you figure out where to go. Certainly there's enough space, and I could use a hand. Not only with the house, but I have some questions for you. Questions about my father."

Her throat tightened. "It's a deal. I'll earn my keep. I promise."

"I'm counting on it. I'm going to head over to the west wing for the night. I can keep an ear open to anyone who might try to come back and cause trouble. Are you okay being in the east wing by yourself?"

Bailey nodded. "Yeah, I'll be fine." She'd sleep with her door locked. Maybe with a dresser pushed in front of it. She might even sneak a kitchen knife into her nightstand.

Even with all of those precautions, she probably still wouldn't get any sleep.

As they stepped inside, Ed paused.

"What is it?"

He shook his head. "Just a gut feeling."

"About what?"

"That someone is coming and going as they please. In a house this size, it's going to be almost impossible to catch them. Not without some equipment, stuff that we don't have."

That thought didn't comfort her as she mumbled good-night to Ed and then trudged up to her room. Once inside, she leaned against the door a moment, trying to control her racing heartbeat.

Something on her coverlet caught her eye.

With trepidation in each of her steps, she approached the bed.

She gasped when she looked down and saw pictures of her and Ed at Samantha's house. Scrawled in red ink across the picture were the words *All play and no work makes Bailey a sad girl.*

SEVEN

Bailey stared at the note, which trembled along with her hands. Another threat. Another reminder of what was expected of her.

She had to step up her game and really search for some answers.

But where? Where else could she look? Where might Mr. Carter have left this mysterious information?

She closed her eyes and pictured the house, visualized every room and place she'd checked already. What was left?

The attic, Bailey realized. It would be the perfect place for Mr. Carter to hide something. She shivered at the thought of going into the dark, rarely used space.

It was easy to forget there was an attic because the access to the space was in a closet in an unused bedroom.

Despite the fear that coursed through her, she knew she had to check up there. That man would make good on his threats if she didn't find the information he'd requested. She couldn't put her sister's life in danger.

Ed was sleeping in the west wing, which meant if she was quiet, he might never have a clue what she was up to.

She shoved a flashlight into her back pocket and picked up a candle. It seemed so old-fashioned to use a candle, but she didn't want to trust only one source of light. The house was incredibly dark. She could only imagine what the attic would be like. She shuddered at the thought.

Quietly, she pulled her door open, checked the hallway to make sure it was clear and then stepped out. She tiptoed toward the last bedroom, slipped inside and froze.

She'd never liked attics. Never. But the thought of going up there now caused panic to claim her entire being.

I can do this, she told herself. *There's nothing to be afraid of. Look for the information and leave.*

Her pep talk did little good.

Lord, be with me. Be a light in this darkness. Drive away my fear.

She opened her eyes and sucked in a deep breath. The light from the candle's flames flickered around the room, casting strange shadows.

Just a lamp. A dresser. A mirror.

No strange, lurking men. No traps.

She trepidly took her first step and then scrambled all the way to the closet door. She pulled it open, and the stale, dusty smell of the attic floated downward.

She gripped the candle and began climbing the stairs, counting each step as she went. Finally, she reached the top. The ache in her throat only intensified.

The steep roof made the space narrow. Without any windows, not even the moon could comfort her. Just the light of her candle. That was all she had.

She closed her eyes again, imagining Jesus as a beacon of light in the night. As a child, she'd loved thinking about being a light in an otherwise dark world. She tried to use her smile, her optimism to brighten people's day. Much like this candle guided her path, she had to tap into a different kind of power inside her. She had to rely on God's strength right now.

She took her first step, the wooden floor creaking underneath her feet.

What was she even looking for? She scanned the area and spotted several old paintings, a dresser, some trunks, random boxes. At the other side, there were two doors. One probably led to another entrance. The other could be a closet, perhaps.

This could take a while.

She set the candle on top of the dresser, wishing she'd thought to bring a few more with her. It was too late to go back now; if she left, she might not come back.

She started with the first box. Nothing. It was filled with various bills that the previous owners had left here. The next three boxes revealed more of the same.

Had Mr. Carter ever been up here even? He'd been mobile up until the last couple of weeks before he died. His health had deteriorated steeply during that time. Being up here might be a dead end, after all.

Still, she moved on to the trunks. She found fascinating old journals and books with yellowed pages and some old family photos, but nothing that screamed "important" or seemed relevant to what she needed.

Standing, she wiped the dust off her legs. For a moment, she'd almost forgotten she was up here. But as she glanced around the space again, she shivered. She couldn't wait to get out of here.

She made her way across the floor. This was her last possibility—an old filing cabinet. If the information wasn't in here, she didn't know where she'd look. She'd be back to square one.

Twenty minutes later, she shoved down another phone bill. The previous owners had been the best record keepers ever. But that didn't help her now.

She pushed aside some dried leaves and a box with rat poison in it. Of course there was nothing underneath. That would have been too easy.

Leaning back, she sighed and blew a hair out of her face. All of this for nothing.

Just as she stood, the candle went dark.

She gasped as absolute darkness surrounded her.

Panic made her feel outside of herself. She scrambled to retrieve her flashlight from her back pocket. Before she could, she sensed movement behind her.

She started to lunge, to dart away, when something sticky hit her face.

A cobweb.

She swatted in front of her, suddenly feeling imaginary spiders all over her skin.

Her flashlight. She had to use her flashlight. She pulled it from her back pocket and fumbled to find the switch.

Her chest heaved in fear. She paused, reassessing the situation. When she heard nothing, she nearly laughed at herself. Had that movement been her imagination? Had she simply let her fear get the best of her?

All those crazy stories she'd read as a child about spooky attics had finally caught up with her. She'd just been overreacting.

Just as she found the on switch to her flashlight, arms gripped her like a vise and a hand covered her mouth.

Ed lay in bed, staring at the ceiling.

He couldn't get Bailey out of his mind. She really did care about his father. That much had become clear today when he'd listened to her talk.

Despite that, he still couldn't figure her out. There was something she wasn't telling him. If her reasons for being here were honest and innocent, then why was she hiding something?

A thump pulled him out of his thoughts.

He sat up with a start. What was that noise?

He threw on his clothes, tucked his gun into his belt and

crept toward the stairway. He wasn't sure if Bailey was causing trouble or if she was in trouble, but that noise had definitely come from inside the residence.

He moved slowly as he cleared the landing. There was no sign of movement in the hallway. Cautiously, he checked each room.

When he reached Bailey's room, he paused. The door was open. Certainly she wouldn't sleep without locking up behind her. Not after everything that had happened.

He stepped in and surveyed the area. The bed was made. Everything appeared untouched, and there was no sign of Bailey.

He paused by something on her bed and picked up a picture. Pulling out his flashlight, he shone it down on the paper.

It was a photo of him and Bailey eating together today. What was that about? Who had taken it?

The sprawling words slashed across the bottom only intensified his unease. *All play and no work makes Bailey a sad girl.*

Something was wrong.

Was this a threat? Or was it a message from someone she was working for?

He couldn't be sure. He wanted to believe Bailey; he really did. But there was so much at stake. He'd learned the hard way not to be too trusting.

A creak sounded above him.

He paused. That didn't come from the roof.

There was someone in the attic, he realized.

Where was the attic? How did he even get there? He needed to figure that out and fast.

"Evidently, I need to prove to you that my threats aren't idle," the man whispered into Bailey's ear.

She struggled, trying to get away. It was useless. Finally, she froze, waiting to hear what the man would say next.

"I do what I say, Bailey. There's no time for these raking leaves, having picnics with friends things. I need that information and I need it now. Perhaps you don't understand the urgency of it all."

She nodded, praying the man would let her go.

"Just in case you're thinking about telling Ed, I wouldn't be too quick to open up to him. And, if you do, we'll know. We have our ways. In fact, I'm thinking it would be a lot easier for you to accomplish your mission without him around here."

Was he saying he meant to kill Ed? The thought made her heart thud dully in her chest.

Also, she just realized he'd said *we*. There was more than one person working with him. Bailey should have known.

"Things will get ugly if you betray us. Do you understand?"

Bailey nodded again.

"Here's a taste of what will happen if you don't hold up your end of the bargain."

He shoved her forward. When her feet dug into the floor, he lifted her. She kicked and flailed, but it was useless.

Something squeaked and the next thing she knew she was tossed against the wall. There was another squeak, a click and then silence.

She shifted, her shoulder aching. She rubbed the skin there and felt the burning at her elbow. She'd probably have a few scrapes and bruises. But she was still alive. For the time being, at least.

All Bailey could see was blackness. The floor was gritty beneath her. Invisible bugs tickled her skin, made her squirm. The dust and stale air took her breath away and sent her into a coughing fit.

The closet, she realized. The man had dumped her in the closet. In the attic.

Did Ed even know there was an attic in the house? Would he come looking for her? Even if he did, it wouldn't be until morning. He wouldn't hear her up here. There was too much space between his bedroom and this closet.

She was trapped here until morning. She couldn't let that thought send her into a panic.

Besides, what did her attacker know about Ed that she didn't? What was Ed hiding?

Tears threatened to spill from her eyes. She just didn't know who she could believe anymore or what to think.

She pushed against the door, hoping foolishly that it was unlocked.

It didn't budge.

Something crawled over her arm and she stifled a scream.

She must have dropped her flashlight when the man grabbed her.

Breathe deep. Stay calm. Don't freak out.

She repeated the instructions over and over, hoping staying focused would ease her panic.

What was she going to do? What if she didn't find the information?

Lord, I feel trapped, and I'm not just talking about this closet. I feel like I'm drowning and there's no hope for rescue, like it's just a matter of time before I go under.

Just then something creaked outside.

Was her attacker coming back? If so, what kind of punishment had he planned this time?

She braced herself. Her heart pounded in her chest.

The door opened and a light shined on her.

"Bailey?" a familiar voice asked.

Ed. It was Ed.

She jerked to her feet and darted from the small space. Despite her resolve to not touch Ed, she found herself reaching for his arm, needing something to anchor her. She'd never been so glad to see the man.

"What are you doing? What happened?" Ed gripped her arms.

She wanted to blurt everything. Then she remembered her attacker's threat, his warning not to tell anyone. Her thoughts collided inside until fear for her sister's safety won out.

"I couldn't sleep. I was cleaning. I…I somehow backed into the closet. The door, well, the door—it locked." Ed was no dummy. Certainly he'd see through her story. He'd hear the tremble in her voice, the uncertainty, and know she was lying.

"You came to the attic to clean? At midnight?"

She nodded. "Strange…habit, I know. I just…I got—got carried away."

Ed eyed her warily. "It's a good thing I heard you, then. Otherwise, you would have been up here all night. Let's get you downstairs."

Her brain kept telling her to release Ed's arm, but she couldn't physically do it. She clutched him as if holding on for dear life as he led her to the stairs. It wasn't until they were back in the hallway that she released her grip.

She straightened and pushed a hair behind her ear, trying to gain some sense of dignity. "Thank you again."

He stared at her. There was something he wanted to say. She could see it in his eyes. But finally he nodded. "No more cleaning, okay?"

"Got it." No, she had much more important matters to attend to, matters that meant life or death.

EIGHT

Bailey didn't remember falling asleep, but she must have because when she woke up, the electricity was working again. She hurried out of bed and into her adjoining bathroom. A warm shower had never felt as good. But not even the soothing water could wash away the memories of being locked in the attic closet last night.

Maybe she should tell Ed what was going on. This was all concerning his father, after all. And even if her attacker had eyes on her at all times, there was still the possibility that he wouldn't be able to hear the conversation they had, especially not if they were isolated—on the beach or on a boat.

Maybe she could call her sister, tell her to get away for a while. She could call the police, the FBI, and let them know what was going on.

Despite those possibilities, she knew that finding the information was paramount. She needed to go through all of Mr. Carter's things to do that, to search the house from top to bottom. Even the places she'd already examined.

She felt as if she would lose her mind if she lived under this pressure for much longer.

Ed was sitting at the kitchen table drinking some coffee when she got downstairs. He looked up and nodded. "Bailey, good morning."

The electricity must have made him a little happier, as well. He'd even shaved. "Good morning."

She poured herself some coffee, relishing the feel of the warm mug at her fingers, before slogging across the room. She lowered herself at the table across from him. Sunlight streaming through the window above the sink heated her cheeks and seemed to promise everything would be okay.

"I was thinking of going into town to see if I can find groceries. Since we're going to be staying and all, we'll need some more to eat. Plus, I think the ferry is running again. The first boat should be here by nine, most likely with supplies. I figure if you're going to go through your father's things, you'll need some boxes to help with organization."

He set his coffee down. "Good idea. I'll go with you."

Was he going with her to help or because he didn't trust her?

"Ed, there's something I wanted to—" She looked toward the distance at something that had been placed on one of the shelves by the kitchen sink. There was something that hadn't been there before. She stood, gravitating toward it with dread in her gut.

"Yes?" Ed asked.

She barely heard him. She stepped closer, squinting. What she saw made her reel. Her pain almost felt physical.

"What is it?" Ed asked, appearing behind her.

She pointed to the picture there. Her finger trembled as her eyes welled with tears. "Did you put that there?"

"Put what there? That photo?"

She nodded.

"Why would I put a photo there?" He leaned closer to examine it. "I don't even know who these people are."

"It's my sister and her kids," Bailey muttered.

In the picture, Lauren was bent over tying Emma's soccer shoes while her son, Alex, watched in the distance.

Bailey closed her eyes. These people were close enough to touch her sister.

She couldn't risk telling Ed anything. It was too big of a chance. One wrong move and everything could fall apart for her.

Ed picked up the picture. "That's kind of strange. There's a date stamp on the bottom that indicates this picture was taken yesterday."

He looked at Bailey, watching her expression carefully, and clearly saw the fear that flickered in her eyes. But why?

"You're saying you didn't put this picture here?" Ed clarified.

Bailey nodded. "That's exactly what I'm saying."

"Then how did it get here?"

"That's what I'm wondering."

Ed pressed his lips together a moment, not liking where this was going. "Where does your sister live?"

"Florida," Bailey answered.

"So, someone took a picture of your sister in Florida yesterday and managed to get the picture here in this house sometime between then and now?"

Bailey looked up at him, her big blue eyes brimming with tears. "I know it sounds crazy. I wish I had some answers. I really do. I have no idea how that picture got here, who took it or why. It's all just really creepy, to say the least."

Ed crossed his arms, his thoughts racing. "I knew it felt like someone had been in the house when we got back yesterday."

"Of all the things someone could break in to do, though." She shook her head.

Ed didn't miss how it seemed as if she'd gone into a trancelike state. She was really shaken up by all of this, and he couldn't blame her. Someone was playing a twisted game, and he was only now beginning to realize what the stakes were. He'd known last night that the incident in the attic was no accident. But was someone threatening her? Had she gotten herself in too deep, become too entangled with the wrong people? Or was she a willing accomplice, playing a game and preying on his goodwill?

He put a hand on Bailey's elbow. "Come on. Let's get out of here. Some fresh air will do us good."

They headed out and started across the grass toward the shed where the bikes were kept. A large barn, original to the property, stood behind the house, though no one except the groundskeeper ever used it.

An hour later they'd bought five bags of groceries and ordered some boxes that should be in by the end of the week. Their trip into town had been surprisingly comfortable. Their chitchat as they traveled to and from had almost seemed familiar and easy.

Bailey had stopped to talk to several people. It was obvious in the short amount of time she'd been on the island that she'd developed a sense of belonging. Ed wondered what that would be like.

He couldn't think that far into the future, though. Right now, he had to focus on finding answers, and he had very little to go on. He'd made some calls and wanted to get to know some people in town, find out who was coming and going.

The picture of Bailey's family lingered in his mind. What did it mean? He wouldn't so easily believe that this was just a coincidence, not with everything that had been going on.

Ed stopped in his tracks when they reached the backside of the house. "We didn't leave that door cracked open."

Bailey's steps slowed. "No, we didn't."

Ed put his bags on the ground and reached into his jacket. "Stay back."

Bailey only stared at him. "A gun? You brought a gun with you to the grocery store?"

He tried to ignore her, but she kept staring. "Do you have a problem with that?"

"What kind of lawyer carries a gun with him everywhere?"

"A lawyer who's always ready for anything. Now, can we stop talking so I can check out the house?" Ed stared at her and saw the fear in her eyes. Did she really think he would hurt her? The thought was unsettling.

She pulled her gaze away from the gun and frowned. "Of course."

He crept up to the house, listening for signs of any suspicious movements or intruders. All was silent.

As he nudged the door open, he scanned the interior of the house. He didn't see anything out of place. The kitchen chairs were as they left them. His coffee mug was still on the table. One of the curtains still hung lopsided. Even the picture of Bailey's sister was still there.

He really didn't want to search this entire house again. But he would if he had to.

Stepping into the kitchen, he noticed Bailey behind him. "I thought I asked you to stay outside."

"Why do we keep going back and forth on this? Stay together, separate. Separating seems like such a bad idea when danger could be close," Bailey said.

"Or you could have just walked into danger," he groused. "Stay here while I check out the house. Please."

She frowned but nodded.

Ed searched but found no one. Strange. Why was that door open, then? Had the wind blown it open?

He shook his head and went back to join Bailey in the kitchen. She was waiting where he'd told her to stand, but she didn't look happy.

It was time they talked. Really talked. He needed to find out what she knew.

"Everything okay?" she asked.

He tucked his gun back into the holster. "I didn't see anything."

He went to the cabinet and pulled out some tea he'd found this morning. He put the kettle on the stove, thankful to finally have power. He didn't want to scare Bailey by bombarding her with questions. He'd take a gentle, more friendly approach by offering to chat over tea.

"I found the canister this morning. It was my dad's favorite. Would you like some?" he asked.

Bailey shook her head. "No, I think I'm going to try to organize your father's things and straighten up a bit. Is that okay?"

Interesting.

Change of plans. Maybe instead of talking, he'd see exactly what she was up to. He'd give her a few minutes and then catch her red-handed.

Bailey paused in the laundry room. It was one of the few rooms that she hadn't searched. It seemed an unlikely place to hide anything, but maybe that would essentially make it the perfect place to stash something of importance.

She started on the top shelf of the cabinet and searched through tubs of cleaners, rags, old batteries and tools. As she looked, she thought about Ed's gun. For a moment when he'd pulled it out earlier, fear had coursed through her.

She had no proof that he was a good guy. And the man last night had warned her that Ed wasn't who she thought. Everyone seemed insistent on playing mind games with her. She couldn't tell which way was up anymore.

She hadn't even finished the first cabinet when her cell

phone buzzed. She climbed from the ladder, wiped the sweat from her brow and leaned against the washer.

A text message was waiting for her.

Maybe your search would be more effective if I got Ed out of the way first.

She gasped. What? Though she'd just been questioning Ed's innocence in all of this, there was no way she wanted someone to die in this twisted game, no matter what side he or she was potentially on.

With trembling fingers, she texted back.

Why don't you just search for yourself? Why do you need me?

She held her breath, waiting for his response, wondering if she should have remained silent. The last thing she wanted was to provoke this man even more.

You're our inside connection.

She started to reply and then froze. Those leaves she'd seen in the attic last night—the ones beside the rat poisoning. Were they…tea leaves? Had someone messed with them and returned them to the kitchen?

Ed was making himself some tea.

With a gasp, she dropped what she was doing and darted toward the kitchen. She reached the tile floor there just as Ed was raising a cup to his lips. Without thinking, she smacked it out of his hands.

The cup flew through the air before smashing against the wall. Shards of porcelain, as well as hot liquid, splattered everywhere.

Ed looked up, an incredulous look in his eyes. "Have you lost your mind?"

Bailey swallowed hard. She hadn't had time to think of any kind of reasonable-sounding explanation. "That tea's bad. Old. No good."

He raised an eyebrow. "Is that right?"

She nodded. "I meant to tell you that earlier. I didn't think about it until just now. I didn't want you to get sick."

"From tea?"

"Nothing worse than bad tea."

"I'm pretty sure tea never goes bad."

Did tea expire? She didn't know and she didn't have time to think about it. "We found bugs in a couple of canisters. I thought I'd thrown out this old stuff already." She grabbed the old tins and dumped them in the trash.

Ed still stared on as though she'd lost her mind. He rose slowly, his gaze laced with skepticism as he started toward the living room. "You know what? I think I'm going to change. Some of that tea splattered on me."

Bailey sat down hard in a kitchen chair. Had she over-reacted? Should she try to send a sample of the tea in to be tested? Where would she even send it? Even if she found somewhere, by the time she got the results back, it would probably be too late.

Fear continued to grow inside her. She couldn't just sit here all day. She had to keep looking for something she wasn't sure she could even identify. Whoever the man was behind this, he was making it obvious that he had eyes on her at all times. It was unnerving.

She stood and took a deep breath, trying to wipe away her frustration. As she stepped back toward the laundry room, a distinct scent caught her nose. What was that … smoke?

She sprinted toward the stairway.

She glanced down the hallways on the first floor and

saw nothing. Taking the steps by two, she darted upstairs. The hallway appeared clear.

Skirting the landing at the center of the house, she reached the west wing.

Smoke.

That was definitely smoke.

And it was coming from...the direction of Ed's room.

NINE

Bailey only took two steps when she spotted the flames. They flickered from Ed's door and grew larger by the minute. Adrenaline surged in her.

This was not going to be the way it all ended. Not if she had anything to do with it. She was a nurse; it was her job to help people, not to leave them in their time of need.

She darted back downstairs, into the laundry room, and grabbed a fire extinguisher she'd seen there while cleaning. Tucking it under her arm, she sprinted back to Ed's room. She wasted no time in spraying the flames.

Finally, any visible flames disappeared, leaving only a faint orange flicker to the black charred wood and a lot of heavy smoke. She had no idea what it looked like inside the room, though.

She jerked off her sweatshirt and wrapped it around her hand before grabbing the doorknob.

Please open.

Thankfully, it did.

She pulled her shirt over her mouth as thick smoke billowed out. Where was Ed? She could hardly see through the thick, gray air.

She pushed her way inside, using the extinguisher to douse more flames.

Despite her shirt, smoke filled her lungs. She swatted the air in front of her, desperately wanting to see.

She spotted Ed, bent over with a hand on his head.

"Come on!" she shouted.

She slipped an arm around his waist and led him out of the room. She didn't stop until they'd reached the end of the hallway. Her shoulder ached, she could hardly breathe, and her head was pounding by the time she lowered Ed to the ground. She sank down there beside him.

"What happened?" she asked.

He nodded, still trying to catch his breath and looking a bit dazed. "Someone hit me over the head. It's the last thing I remember before waking up with flames around me and then seeing you."

"I've got to call 911. You going to be okay?"

He nodded again, sucking in a raspy breath. "Yeah, I'll be fine."

She grabbed her phone and dialed, knowing things could have turned out much worse.

"We won't know for sure until the fire marshal investigates, but it looks to me like an electrical fire that started between the walls," Sheriff Davis said. The man was probably in his early thirties with curly blond hair and blue eyes. Bailey had insisted that he was trustworthy, but Ed remained leery of most people.

Should he tell the sheriff that someone knocked him out before the fire happened? Or would that raise too many questions? The last thing he wanted was people poking into his business.

"An electrical fire, huh?" Ed ran a hand over his face.

The sheriff nodded. "Not unusual in older homes. With the power just being restored, there could have been a surge. Anyway, it's a good thing you got out when you did and that Bailey thought to hit the breaker. When the fire marshal gets here, he'll be able to tell you whether it's safe to sleep here in the residence."

Just then, a shadow filled the doorway. Ed looked back and saw Henry Wilkins there. The man had been the groundskeeper here for many years. His wife had recently become ill and he'd drastically cut back his hours. He was in his late sixties with thin light brown hair, a protruding gut and at least three chins.

Ed had called the man this morning and asked him to stop by and take a look at the window. Plus, he wanted to talk to Henry, see if he knew anything. "I heard there was trouble and headed over here early," he said. He glanced up, where smoke still clung to the ceiling. "Looks like more than a window that will need to be fixed."

"If you'll excuse me, I'm going to go file my report." The sheriff slipped away. "I'd stay out of that wing of the house until we know if there's any structural damage."

"Will do," Ed said.

Ed and Henry chatted about the fire for several minutes before Wilkins turned toward Bailey. "I meant to tell you, a man stopped by the other day looking for you."

Bailey raised her eyebrows. "A man?"

He nodded. "Said he was trying to find you. That was the day you went over for the funeral. I couldn't make it because my wife was feeling especially ill. I stopped by here for just a moment to grab some tools before heading home."

"No one's been in contact with me since then," Bailey said, shaking her head. "What did he look like?"

Wilkins shrugged. "I figured he was an old boyfriend or something. He was tall and big. Not like fat big, but weight-lifting big. He had a bit of an accent. It was slight, but it was there. He had dark, curly hair, a cleft chin, and maybe he was Middle Eastern or from India? I'm not sure."

"Doesn't sound familiar."

"Either way," Wilkins continued. "He said he was going to be back. Something about picking up something that you have for him? I'm sorry I forgot to mention it. I've had so much on my mind lately."

Ed could read the emotions washing over Bailey. Surprise, confusion, fear.

What was she scared of? Something lurked beneath the surface. He had to figure out what. She'd saved his life, but her earlier behavior was so peculiar.

"Wilkins, have you noticed anything strange going on around here lately?"

The older man rubbed his chin. "I did see a boat outside at your dad's pier a week or so ago."

His instincts spiked. John had mentioned the same thing. "Really? What were the people on board doing?"

"I figured they pulled up thinking the place was abandoned or something, so I shooed them off."

"Did they say anything?" Ed asked.

"Naw. Not much. Just apologized and went on their way. It was a guy and a girl. Couldn't tell much about them. Both were wearing hats."

"Is that unusual?" Ed continued.

Wilkins shrugged again. "Wouldn't say so. People come from all over to see this island. They think it's the place where time stood still. People just get curious. This house, of course, stands out. It's about ten times the size of the rest."

"It is a big one. You would know that better than anyone, since you've been keeping the grounds up for...for how long now?"

"Nearly twenty years. Even before your father bought the place. I've been coming twice a week to cut the grass, trim the bushes and pull the weeds. Can't do some of the other stuff anymore. But I can find people who can." Wilkins fixated on Ed a moment. "You going to stay here?"

Ed shrugged. "I don't know yet what I'm doing, Mr.

Wilkins. The idea is tempting, I suppose. I'm not sure is-land life is for me, though."

"Stay here long enough and you'll realize that it is. The slower pace does a body good." He turned toward Bailey. "How about you?"

"I've got to figure things out. I'll probably look for an-other job as a home health nurse and see where that takes me."

"You could help Doc Jennings out," he suggested.

"I hardly think the island needs a doctor *and* a nurse."

"Rumor has it he wants to retire and move down to Texas to be with his son and grandkids."

She shrugged. "Tempting, but who knows if that will happen or when it will happen. I'm just trying to wrap everything up here."

He glanced back at Ed. "You want me to take a look at that window?"

Ed nodded. "That would be great. If you can't fix it, if you could point me in the direction of someone who can, that would be great. I'll show you where it happened."

They started walking toward the kitchen when Bailey called to him and motioned him over. For a moment—and just a moment—he wondered what it would be like if she was calling him over for some reason other than all the craziness happening lately. What it would be like if the two of them were a couple enjoying time together.

Then he realized that the thought was crazy. No matter how hard he might want the possibility.

TEN

Bailey leaned against the wall as Ed walked away. She folded her arms across her chest, trying to get her pulse back down to a more stable rate.

She didn't care what the chief said. She knew the truth. Someone had started that fire—tampered with the wiring maybe—and made it look like an accident. The person behind the crime probably hadn't intended to kill Ed, but he was trying to send a message, one that Bailey heard loud and clear. No one was safe.

These guys weren't afraid to take action, to claim lives.

And who was the man Henry had mentioned who'd stopped by? Had someone scoped her out before the funeral even ended? The man certainly didn't fit the description of any of her exes. Besides that, none of them knew she was here on Smuggler's Cove.

There had only been one thing to comfort her in the past hour, and that was the fact that Mr. Wilkins recognized Ed. From the way they talked, it sounded as though Ed *had* been here before. That he'd been here quite often before. That didn't fit with Bailey's theories about him, though. And if that was the case, why hadn't he been here when it was most important—at the end of his dad's life?

Everything about the man seemed secretive and mysterious, as if he was hiding matters of national security behind those blue eyes. Those incredibly mesmerizing blue eyes. Blue eyes she could lose herself in forever.

She shook her head. She couldn't think like that. Not only did Ed Carter suspect she might be responsible for killing his father, but he was also everything she didn't want in a man. She'd come here to get away from his type. She needed someone who didn't have aspirations of corporate ladders and a fast-paced lifestyle. She needed someone who wasn't always looking for greener pastures and who appreciated the small things in life. She didn't see that a lot in career-oriented guys.

Ed had proven that was his mind-set in his halfhearted answer to Wilkins about whether or not he would move here.

If Bailey were smart, she'd get off the island and run, not look back. But then she thought about her sister, and her sister's kids, and her sister's husband, Jason, who was out to sea with the navy right now. They were the picture of what Bailey wanted.

Lauren had stopped working so she could homeschool her children. The family did without expensive cable and fancy vacations, instead choosing to go hiking or do service projects together so they could afford to live on one income. Instead of taking dance class or playing sports through pricey studios or clubs, they utilized classes offered at local community centers. They were some of the kindest, sweetest, most loving people Bailey knew—and she wasn't just saying that because they were family.

The greater fact remained that she couldn't put the people she loved in danger.

With Henry and Ed out of earshot, she pulled out her phone and called her sister.

Relief filled Bailey when she heard Lauren's sweet, soft voice.

"You doing okay?" Bailey asked in a rush. She continued to scan everything around her, looking for a sign of trouble or an intruder or anything else that might signal danger. All she saw was some leftover smoke lingering in the air.

Her sister laughed. "Of course I'm doing okay. Why do you sound so worried? I should be the one asking you that after that storm just hit that dinky island where you've been living."

"I'm fine. The storm could have been worse, in all honesty. I didn't hear from you for a few days, so I was concerned."

"We've just been running around. Between all the kids' activities, I've hardly had a moment to think."

Bailey's heart slowed. "Okay. Good. That's what I wanted to hear."

"Everything okay? You don't sound like yourself."

"I'm good," Bailey insisted. Now that she knew Lauren was okay, she needed to get off the phone before too many questions were asked. "Listen, I've got to go. I'll call soon, though. Tell the kids Aunt Bailey said hello!"

Four hours later, the fire marshal finally cleared the house. He advised everyone to stay out of the west wing until repairs were made, but he saw no immediate danger.

As soon as he left, Ed turned to Bailey. "I don't think I've said thank-you yet. What you did when you found me in that room was brave."

"Nothing you wouldn't do."

He wanted to ask about the tea, about the picture he'd found on her bed, about her suspicious behavior. But how could he really accuse someone who'd just saved him?

He needed to handle this carefully. "Bailey, I—"

Just then, Ed's cell phone rang, and he recognized his friend's number. "I've got to take this."

He excused himself and walked down the east wing

for some privacy. They'd have to finish that conversation later. "What's going on, Archie?"

Archie was one of the best tech ops that Ed had known. They'd worked together on several missions, and Ed knew he could trust him. He'd kept the details of his time here quiet to everyone else—even his boss—until he knew who was on his side. If anyone could help Ed find the answers, it was him.

"Any updates?" Archie asked. "I haven't heard from you in a few days and wanted to make sure you didn't have two feet in the grave."

"You should know me better than that, Archie. I make every effort to only have one foot in the grave at a time."

His friend laughed. "Of course."

"No real updates here." Ed glanced behind him, making sure Bailey wasn't listening. "Something was definitely going on with my father. His death wasn't from natural causes."

"When are you going to send me his medication?" Archie asked.

"I have someone stopping by on Thursday to pick it up. They'll take it right to you so you can test it."

"If you're right and someone did mess with his prescriptions, do you have any idea who might have switched the pills?" Archie asked.

"The most likely suspect would be his nurse."

"Do you think she's capable of that? That she's working for the other side?"

Ed locked his jaw in place for a moment as he remembered Bailey's kind eyes. "I don't know yet. That's what I'm trying to figure out."

"There's one more thing I wanted to tell you." Archie paused. "Sanderson has disappeared."

Ed's muscles tightened. "What do you mean, disappeared?"

"He somehow managed to slip away from our surveillance. No one knows where he is. I just wanted you to know."

Sanderson was only one of the most dangerous terrorists of this century. Part of Ed's deep-cover assignment had been to tail the man. Sanderson was a former British intelligence operative. Now he didn't work for any side; he simply worked for himself, doing whatever he could to ensure he had more power and more wealth.

The man was dangerous. He had an army of followers and together they'd planned terror attacks in several different countries. The most recent one had taken place in Libya, where six Americans with diplomatic ties were killed. Most of the public didn't realize the true implications of the acts; they wouldn't sleep knowing what the true stakes were.

Classified information had been stolen before the bomb engaged, which was what claimed so many lives—twenty altogether. That information was held as leverage over the Libyian government as well as the government of the Ukraine. Both countries had eased sanctions, knowing if the intel was released into the public that outrage would ensue—outrage that could topple a government.

"I'll keep you updated on what I find out," Archie said. "I just thought you should know. In theory, this man should have no idea what your real identity is. In reality…well, you know what that's like."

Archie was right. Sanderson shouldn't have any idea who Ed really was. He'd posed as an equities trader while trying to gather information on the man. The assignment had been his life for the past several months. As part of his job, he'd worked with one of Sanderson's right-hand men. He'd recorded how they came and went. He observed who they spent time with. He reported when they took trips out of the country.

He'd pulled out of the assignment when he'd finally learned of his father's death. He'd been under what was called deep cover, which meant essentially that his entire life was erased. His job became his new life, and his new identity became his only reality.

The only reason he'd been notified of his father's death was because the government suspected something was amiss. Of course Ed was the most logical person to figure out what that was. But he was here now unofficially. He'd told the CIA that he needed to take some time to sort through everything, to grieve. He'd been telling the truth. He wouldn't rest until his father had justice.

Until he knew who was clear, he had a handful of people he trusted and truly considered friends at the CIA right now. They were the only ones he'd ask to help him.

When he returned to the living room, Bailey was kneeling in front of the fire, seemingly mesmerized by the flames.

The image made him pause. She looked so serene, yet pensive. He had the strange desire to rub her back, to tell her everything would be okay. He didn't know her story, but at the moment she seemed so alone.

She glanced up, startled almost, as he got closer. A sad smile briefly played on her lips. "Hey."

He pulled a chair up and sat beside her. "You doing okay?"

Surprise fluttered through her gaze until she finally nodded. "I'm hanging in. It was a crazy day. A crazy week, for that matter. I had no idea when I accepted this assignment that it would turn into this."

Her words caused him to bristle. Assignment? What exactly was she saying?

She continued, "I wasn't sure if home health care was for me, but I treasured being able to be there for someone during their final moments."

He nearly laughed at himself. Her assignment here with his father. Of course. He had to stop thinking like a spy.

"Why'd you really come here, Bailey? Why the career change?"

Her gaze remained fixed on the fire. "A lot of reasons. A lot of signals telling me it was time for a change. I'd worked in the ER for a long time. The pace was hectic, frantic. It worked for me for a while, but I was getting tired. I guess what sealed the deal for me was Bobby."

"Who was Bobby?"

"A rising executive with a local advertising firm down in Raleigh. I realized that his career was his first love and that I'd always be second place. Then I looked around and realized that most of the people I knew had different priorities than I did. Life was about money and success. I count my success in my relationships, in the moments. I mean, most of the people I knew never said that exactly, but their actions spoke loudly. I knew I wanted more. I wanted a slower pace."

"Slower paces are nice, and you don't get much slower than around here."

She nodded. "In the middle of all of that, my own father became ill. He was diagnosed with heart disease and died two months later. I stayed with him, taking care of him during his final days. My mom passed away when I was sixteen, so my sister and I were all he had. I realized how important those final moments in life can be. That's why I chose hospice."

Some of the pieces began clicking into place. That was why she was judging him as she did. She'd sacrificed her career in order to put her family first, and she thought that Ed couldn't even give up enough time for a funeral.

He had the strange desire to tell her the truth—the whole truth. He wanted to spill everything about how he hadn't found out about his father's death until two days after the fact.

He wanted to tell her how much he mourned his father, how much he'd do anything to go back and spend more time with him, how he already missed his father's wisdom and example.

Certainly, in Bailey's mind, Ed was just like her ex-boyfriend: someone whose career was the most important thing in life. That was how he'd operated for so long now. But for a while his gut had been telling him that he needed to make some changes. Maybe being here on Smuggler's Cove would help things to become clear.

"Being with someone in his or her dying moment is a noble calling, Bailey," he finally said. And he meant it. He'd been with enough people as they'd taken their final breaths. It was gut-wrenching.

"It's hard, but I really felt like it was a ministry."

"You're a believer?" Surprise, maybe even a touch of delight, washed through him.

She nodded. "I wouldn't get through my job without faith. I try to pass that on to my clients. Usually, when people are faced with death, their eyes are opened to things beyond the temporary. They really want to believe that life extends beyond this earth."

His throat went dry. "How about my father?"

"He had a lot of questions at the end. He started going to church. The pastor came by to visit him some. He really turned his life around, Ed. He started reading his Bible."

Joy spread through his soul. Those were the conversations he regretted not having. "That's great."

Bailey looked over at him and smiled. "I know. I didn't realize faith was important to you."

If she knew some of the things he'd seen, she'd know why faith was the only thing that kept him going.

He finally settled on saying, "Your faith is admirable."

"My faith in God is stronger than ever. My faith in people…well, it leaves a lot to be desired."

"Not everyone is like your ex-boyfriend," he said. But even as the words left his mouth, he knew he couldn't put himself in that category. He'd been married to his work. Once he figured out who killed his father, he'd return to the job, to another assignment, to a new group of people.

He was practically a nomad. There was no way to really put down roots in his line of work. For so long, he'd been fine with that. When had something inside him started to change?

Maybe it was after he'd read Romans 12:2 on a card he'd found in his wallet. Because of protocol, he shouldn't have had it there. But someone in the train station had handed it to him. He'd shoved it in his pocket, and somehow it got wedged into his wallet.

Do not conform to the pattern of this world, but be transformed by the renewing of your mind. Then you will be able to test and approve what God's will is—His good, pleasing and perfect will.

It was the word *transformed* that caught his attention. He'd read that verse probably a million times before. But something about reading it then, something about the thought of being transformed—not into someone the CIA wanted him to be, but into someone God wanted him to be—started to nudge at his conscience.

The memories slipped away as Bailey stood and rubbed her hands on her jeans.

"I think I'm going to turn in for the evening. I left a sandwich on the table for you."

"Thank you," he told her.

She slipped off to bed.

He stood, stretching. Maybe he should get his mind off everything by doing some reading. Sometimes just clearing his head for an hour helped him to see things more clearly.

He walked over to the bookshelf and examined some of the titles there. There were plenty of international thrillers and several classics.

What will it be? Grisham or Dickens? he asked himself.

He picked up a title when something caught his eye.

He plucked up a small piece of plastic.

Only it just wasn't a piece of plastic.

It was a hidden camera. Had someone been watching their every move all along?

ELEVEN

Bailey woke the next morning and sat up in bed. She had hardly slept a wink last night. She'd had too much on her mind. Plus, despite the electricity being on, the house was freezing.

Aside from her normal worries, she hadn't been able to stop thinking about her conversation with Ed. He'd showed a surprisingly human side to himself and broken some of the stereotypes she'd placed on him.

What if he did have a good reason for missing his dad's funeral? She couldn't imagine what it might be, but Ed had looked truly mournful that he hadn't been here for his father.

She also wondered what his story was. DC lawyer? There was more to him than that. Maybe he was former military or doing such high-profile work that he'd been threatened. Would that explain why he carried a gun? Why he seemed to know so much about self-defense and bombs?

He still hadn't explained why he thought his father had been murdered, though. Mr. Carter had said some strange things, but at the time Bailey thought he'd just been talking crazy. What if he hadn't been?

But why would someone want to murder someone like Mr. Carter? He was retired, trying to enjoy life. He'd been a number cruncher and, even though she'd joked with Ed about it, why would someone feel the need to kill a number cruncher? It didn't make sense.

Finally, she threw her legs out of bed, got dressed and padded downstairs. As she started toward the kitchen, she noticed Ed sitting in front of the fire. He stared at something in his hands, something small, the size of a coin.

She paused and finally decided to approach him. He didn't even look up as she walked his way, which only increased her curiosity.

"Good morning," she finally said.

He continued to stare at the gadget in his hands. "Good morning."

"Everything okay?"

Finally, he glanced at her, a new hardness in his eyes. "You ever seen this before?"

She squinted at the object, leaning closer. "I don't even know what this is."

"It's a camera. It was hidden on the shelf."

Her hand instinctively went to the bruises at her neck. She could still feel the man's hands there, squeezing, as he threatened her. "Why would there be a camera on the shelf?"

She knew the answer: someone was monitoring her. Who knew where else there were recording devices? They could have planted some on Bailey, for all she knew. With technology as advanced as it was in today's society, a listening device could be a small as a pin tip, she guessed.

"You tell me."

She took a step back. "What sense would it make for me to record myself while I was here?"

He straightened, his aloofness returning at full force. "If not you, then who? Who came to visit my father in his final days? Anyone?"

She shook her head. "The usual, I suppose. Mary Lou. Henry Wilkins. The pastor from the church down the road.

Samantha stopped by with some freshly baked bread. A cousin came by. I'm not sure he ever said his name."

Ed's eyes widened. "Did my father invite his cousin here or did he show up unexpected?"

"I don't think your father invited him. He seemed surprised and asked me to give him some privacy, though."

"And you did?"

"Of course I did. Did you think I'd eavesdrop?"

When he didn't immediately respond, Bailey knew what his answer was. She seethed inwardly. Just last night she'd begun to think he was halfway human. She'd been wrong.

She stared at him, irritation rising in her. "You really think that I not only listened in on your dad's conversations, but that I put cameras around the house? Why would I do that?"

He shook his head. "No, but I think you know more than you're letting on."

So much for the progress that seemed to have happened last night in their strained relationship. She had to turn this conversation around before all the headway they'd made disappeared.

"Look, Ed, maybe we should stop arguing and start working together. We both cared about your father. Working against each other isn't doing either of us any favors."

He stared at her before nodding. "Maybe you're right."

She lowered herself onto the chair across from him, still feeling prickly from his accusations. "Can you tell anything from the camera? Is it still recording?"

"No, I disabled it. It's pretty generic looking. I'd have to send it to a lab for more testing."

"Did you check for any more cameras in the house?"

"I was up for most of the night trying to sweep the place. I found three other recording devices."

Ed looked tired. He had slight circles under his eyes,

his hair was tousled and he was obviously irritable. He was going to make himself sick if he didn't get some rest.

"Who would do this?" The man who'd threatened her would. But who was he? And why? Even more: If Ed knew the answers to those questions, would he tell her?

"I have no idea. I was hoping you might be able to help."

"What if…what if those cameras were planted after your father died? There were lots of guests in and out during that time." She could broach this carefully, without giving anything away.

"Why would someone do that?" Ed tilted his head, seeming intense and focused.

"Someone's obviously looking for something. Isn't that why the library was turned upside down? Maybe someone planted those bugs, hoping to be alerted if we discovered whatever it is they're trying to get their hands on."

Something flickered in his gaze. Was it admiration? "You could be right."

She rubbed her hands on her jeans, trying to cover her unease. "So, what now?"

"Now I'm going to send this camera to a lab."

"You have a lab?"

"As a lawyer, I have a lot of sources I can use for research."

She leaned closer. "Since we're talking about working together now and everything, why don't you just admit that you're not just a lawyer."

Ed's expression remained unchanged. "What do you mean?"

"You're a lawyer for the government, aren't you?"

He didn't say anything for a moment until he finally nodded. "I am. That's why I couldn't be here for the funeral. The case I was working on was an issue of international concern. The ramifications of me leaving in the middle of things would have been devastating. And I don't say that lightly."

At least she'd gotten one thing right. "Sounds serious."

He nodded. "Very. And complicated."

"Life has a way of being complicated."

"How about we try to make it uncomplicated? Let's go into town and talk to some people. This island is small enough that if strangers have been hanging around, someone would have seen them. We need to get to the bottom of what's going on here," Ed offered.

Bailey smiled. "Sounds like a plan."

Before they could stand, the doorbell rang.

Ed pulled the door open and saw the thirtysomething man standing there. The man wore jeans, had one hand tucked into his pocket, and his expression showed confusion.

Perhaps this was the man claiming to be his father's cousin? His father didn't have any cousins, so whoever had come used that as a cover.

"Can I help you?" Ed asked.

"I was looking for Bailey, actually."

Ed stepped back to give Bailey a better view. Her eyes narrowed when she spotted the man there. "Todd? I thought you were gone."

"My mom is all better after her car accident. I decided to come back here and see the storm damage." He held out a stuffed animal. "I found this on your doorstep, by the way."

Bailey's face went pale. "Oh…uh, thanks. I don't know how that—how that got there."

Ed's eyes narrowed. What a strange reaction. She recognized that stuffed animal. Was it hers? If so, why wasn't she saying so?

The man—Todd, Bailey said—glanced at Ed and extended his hand. "Todd Blakely."

"Ed Carter."

"Bill's son?" Todd said, some of his coolness dissolving. "Nice to meet you."

"Todd helped repair the pier, as well as a few other things on the property, until his mom broke her leg in a car crash," Bailey explained. "He went back to Delaware to be with her."

Ed remembered reading about Todd. He'd done background checks on all of the people his father employed, just to be safe. Todd was former navy, had been out for five years, and he'd taken on various jobs as a contractor. His record seemed squeaky-clean enough. Ed couldn't help but wonder what his relationship with Bailey had been. He tried to tell himself that he didn't care, but something about the thought of the two of them being together bothered him.

And made him dislike Todd.

"Come on in," Ed offered, remembering his manners.

Todd shook his head and took a step back. "I don't want to impose. I only wanted to check and make sure everything was okay." He glanced beyond Ed at Bailey. "Maybe we can catch up sometime?"

Bailey nodded, hugging the teddy bear close to her. "Sure thing. I'm not sure how much longer I'm going to be around."

"Let me know before you go, okay? I mean, if you wouldn't mind."

"I'll do that." She nodded, but her expression was still grim.

Todd waved before turning and starting down the path leading away from the house.

Ed waited until he was out of earshot before turning to Bailey. "Friend?"

She nodded and set the stuffed animal on a chair. "Just a friend. I can see your wheels turning."

"I never make assumptions." Not about romance, at least. He was making a lot of assumptions about that bear. If she wanted to tell him, she would. But he had to bite his tongue not to say anything or ask any questions.

They stepped out of the house and started toward town.

"We got to know each other some when he was fixing up your dad's place," Bailey said. "Mr. Wilkins hired him several times, but that's as far as it went. I had the feeling Todd wanted more."

Ed resisted a chuckle. "Had the feeling? I can confirm by the way he looked at you that your suspicions were correct. The man obviously wasn't happy to see me here today."

Bailey shook her head as she tucked her hands into her pockets. "I think you're reading too much into it. Besides, I'm not anxious to date anyone."

He raised his eyebrows, surprised at her hesitancy. "Why's that?"

"I'd rather be single for the rest of my life than be with the wrong person. I'm happy." She shrugged, dragging her feet a little. "I mean, at least for the most part. Of course there's a part of me that would like to settle down somewhere permanent and have kids—like my sister did. But after you get burned a few times by bad relationships you start becoming a skeptic."

"I see."

She glanced at him, shielding her eyes against the sunlight. "You ever been married?"

He shook his head. "Almost." Now, why had he shared that? He hardly ever talked about Claire, especially not with practical strangers like Bailey.

"What happened?" Her eyes lit with curiosity.

That was exactly what he didn't want.

The day was warmer and the waters had gone down some from the storm. Still, the sand was wet at their feet as they walked toward Erma's. "What can I say? She broke my heart and left it in a million pieces."

"Is it still in a million pieces?" She glanced up at him, her expression bordering on adorable.

"The damage just might be irreparable. But it's better that way." It was. He'd learned his lesson the hard way. It wasn't something he'd easily forget.

Bailey frowned. "Why? Because you can have more time on your job that way?"

He wasn't trying to impress anyone, but the criticism in Bailey's voice got to him for some reason. "It's not that I want my job to be my life, but it's hard to find balance. It's hard to take steps back."

"So, why don't you just do it? Make changes? It sounds hard, but that's only in theory. In reality, taking steps back is as simple as saying no. Establishing boundaries. Becoming proactive with your life instead of vice versa."

He glanced over at her. She walked along casually, her hands in the pockets of her white zip-up sweater. Her hair blew in the breeze, and he was struck again by her natural beauty. "You're probably right."

"Of course, you need to consider that the person giving you this advice is jobless and without a home or any roots at all for that matter." She flashed him a wide, self-deprecating smile.

He smiled also, feeling some of his walls come down. It was something he hadn't felt in a long time—the prospect of letting someone in. "Things will look up for you, Bailey."

"I know I'll find another job. Have another encounter with someone else as they're facing death. I have this restless feeling in my chest, like maybe there's something more for me. I just don't have any idea what that something is."

"You said you're a person of faith. Pray about it. You'll get an answer."

She glanced up at him, slowing her steps for a moment. "You surprise me sometimes, Ed."

He raised his eyebrows as an emotion close to delight spread through him. "Do I?"

She nodded. "You do. You're…you're different than I thought you'd be. I'm sorry if I was harsh when we first met."

"If you can overlook me accusing you of my father's murder, then I suppose I can overlook you thinking I'd broken into the house."

They both let out a laugh, the sound nervous and strained, but honest. The restaurant came into view just down the lane.

"Let's see if there's any food left," Ed said.

He had the strangest urge to reach out and grab her hand. Of course, he didn't do it. There was too much at risk. There was no way he could put his heart at risk, as well.

TWELVE

Bailey and Ed grabbed some sandwiches, chips and sodas at Erma's. Her usual menu was on hold until life—and their shipments—resumed to normal following the storm. The day felt balmy, so Bailey and Ed decided to take their sack lunches outside, where they sat on a bench near the piers and dug into their lunch.

Despite the pleasant weather, Bailey's mind kept going to the stuffed bear. That was Alex's bear. Bailey had bought it for him herself. Someone had been close enough to her sister that they'd grabbed the toy.

As if the man's threats didn't seem serious enough, he had to keep reminding her of how dire the situation was.

It had worked. Her nerves were frayed. She was on the edge of having a nervous breakdown. And she didn't know how much longer she could do this.

She cleared her throat, trying to get a grip, trying not to show how raw her emotions were. She needed to stick to logic right now and try to find some answers.

"So, can you please tell me why you think your dad was murdered? I'm really flummoxed that you think that. I was there, Ed." Bailey took a long sip of her soda as she waited for his response.

He frowned, his sandwich raised to his mouth. "Let's just say that someone passed on some information to me that strongly implied that my father's life was on the line."

She stared at him, waiting for him to say more, to offer more of an explanation. When he silently munched on his sandwich instead, she decided that wasn't good enough.

"Who gave you the information implying that?" she pressed.

He put his sandwich down and looked into the distance. "About a week before he died, a friend of his sent me a message implying that something was going on."

"Yet you didn't contact your father until after he died?" She really wanted to understand, but she was having a hard time.

His lips pressed together. "I was out of the country, in a place where I couldn't be easily contacted. I didn't get the message from my father's friend, nor did I get the news of my father's death until five days ago. I came back as soon as I found out."

"Out of the country? Vacation?"

He shook his head. "Work."

"Do you always travel out of the country as a lawyer?" She didn't want to drop this; she wanted answers.

"International law is my specialty."

She raised an eyebrow. "In places so remote you have no contact with the outside world?"

He turned toward her. "I'm not asking you to understand, Bailey. I'm just telling you like it is. It may not be pretty, but it's what I do."

She decided to drop that particular subject. But she did have more questions that had the potential to be equally as uncomfortable.

She wiped her mouth, making sure there was no peanut butter there. "What exactly did your father's friend say that made you so suspicious?"

"It's complicated, Bailey." He looked at her, sorrow in his eyes.

For a moment, her heart panged with compassion.

"Maybe I can help you figure this out. If someone hurt your father, then I want to see justice served, as well."

He stared at her a moment before nodding slowly. "My father's friend was Elmer Martin."

"Elmer? I know Elmer."

His eyebrows shot up. "Do you?"

Bailey nodded. "He came to visit…about a week before your father died." She felt the blood drain from her face as she realized the possible implications of what she said. The visit had seemed so innocent at the time. But what if there were more to it?

"Do you remember anything about his visit?" Ed's eyes suddenly seemed more alert, his body language like someone ready to pounce.

Bailey tried to remember anything of value. She finally shook her head. "Not really. He showed up. We hadn't been planning on him being here, but your father had offered an open invitation to him in the past. I stayed with them for the first hour or so. I brought tea and made sandwiches for them. Then they started catching up about work, and your father told me I could have some free time, that Elmer would keep an eye on him. It seemed innocent at the time."

"I see."

"Do you think Elmer was the killer?" She hardly wanted to ask the question. The man had seemed kind enough. He was an older gentleman, small in stature, but big in spirit.

Ed shook his head. "Elmer died two days before my father."

Her mouth dropped open as she sucked in a deep breath. "What? Are you serious?"

"Unfortunately, yes. It was a boating accident. Tell me this. Did Elmer bring anything with him?"

Bailey tried to remember what the man had looked like when he showed up at the door. She shook her head. "I only remember him wearing a windbreaker type of jacket.

I don't remember any bags or anything. That's probably not very helpful."

"How did he get here?"

"He came over on his boat. By himself. Said he lived up in Maryland."

Ed finished the last of his chips and crumpled the bag. "That's true."

"Ed, where is all of this going?" Her worry—and curiosity—continued to grow.

"I wish I knew, Bailey. I really do."

"And what's this information you've mentioned? What do you think he may have brought with him?" Was this her chance to get to the bottom of all of this? Maybe she could find the answers and put all of this behind her. Maybe she could actually sleep at night, finally knowing that Lauren and her family were safe.

Ed tugged at the collar of his black leather coat. "It had something to do with their work, I think. I only got a message but was never able to talk to Elmer."

"Did you contact anyone with the State Department? Maybe your father's former boss or something? Or did you talk to Elmer's family?"

He frowned, his gaze fixated on something in the distance. "Yes to both of those questions. You have to understand that I had to tread very carefully. I don't have a frame of reference as to what the message was pertaining to."

She could read between the lines. "In other words, you think maybe someone at the State Department could have been involved?" She paused. "I thought your dad was an accountant."

"Like I said, it's complicated."

"Make it uncomplicated."

His jaw hardened. "I wish I could."

She let out a long sigh and raked a hand through her

wind-tangled hair. Frustration spread in her. "I don't know what to say, then."

Ed turned toward her, his eyes soft yet conflicted. "Bailey, I know you hardly know me, but I need you to trust me. There are things I can't talk about."

Her jaw hardened this time. She didn't want to be played as a fool. "International-lawyer type of things?"

"State Department type of things."

Bailey tried to put it all together in her head, but everything seemed too vague. She wished the answers were as simple as the blue sky and as clear as the bay on a windless day. Maybe asking for that was asking too much. "I'm guessing your dad was more than a number cruncher."

"He had a high-level security clearance."

Her throat tightened. "I see."

Ed shifted to better face her. "Bailey, where did my father get his prescriptions filled? Specifically, his heart medicine."

"Well, the island only has one doctor, and he usually comes three times a week. There's no pharmacy here. Most people go over to the mainland to one of the pharmacies there. Most residents take a weekly trip to get everything they can't get here."

"Who picked up those prescriptions for him?"

"I did a lot a lot of times. But Mary Lou, the house-keeper, she picked up supplies for us sometimes."

"Who picked up his last batch of medications?"

"I did." Suddenly, she realized Ed's implications. "You think someone switched out his medication." She swung her head back and forth vehemently. "That's not possible. I was the only one who had access to it."

"That you know of," Ed interjected. "I'm sure you didn't keep the medications on you all the time, did you?"

She shook her head, sobering. "No, they were in your father's bedroom, locked in his drawer."

"How many times did you leave the house after you picked up that batch of medications?"

She searched her memory. "None. I didn't leave at all after that. Not until after your father died."

"Someone either switched them at the pharmacy or switched him here at the house."

"Why are you so certain the medication was switched?" Bailey couldn't understand where he was coming from with all of this. She tried to follow his logic, but jumping to the worst conclusions possible just wasn't in her nature.

"One of the first things I did when I came here was to send off his medications. The results were in my inbox just today."

What? When did he do that? How did I miss it?

Where was Ed getting these resources? Exactly who was he? Something still wasn't adding up.

Yet her gut told her she could trust him.

She just hoped her gut wasn't terribly wrong.

She looked around. They were essentially alone. She wanted to pour out the whole story. The man who threatened her would never know...would he?

Bailey suddenly bristled as she sensed someone watching them. She couldn't shake the feeling, even though every time she looked around, she didn't notice anyone looking their way.

All around them were dockworkers and other people milling around, picking up deliveries from the mainland. Bailey waved at the island's doctor and a couple of people she knew from church.

She glanced toward one of the piers and saw a man staring at her. He turned away and continued to push a broom on the dock. Was he the source of her uneasiness?

She stared at him some more, hoping for a clue as to who he was. He was tall, maybe in his thirties or forties.

He wore a baseball cap over his eyes and a heavy sweat-shirt. But he almost looked like… No, it couldn't be.

But what if it was?

She nudged Ed. "Do you recognize that man?"

He looked up and shook his head. "No. Should I?"

"I'm getting a strange vibe from him. Could be noth-ing. He almost—almost—looks like your father's cousin."

Ed's intense gaze remained on him. "Let's keep an eye on him."

Just then, the man glanced back over. When he saw both Ed and Bailey looking at him, he dropped his broom and took off in a sprint.

Ed jetted after him.

Bailey took a few steps, but knew the chase would be futile. She'd never been a particularly fast runner. But she hated the thought of something happening to Ed, and no one being there.

She quickened her pace, at least trying to keep the two men in her sight.

But they were fast. In what seemed like the blink of an eye, both were gone, disappearing in the direction of the town.

Her hands went to her hips, and she lifted up a prayer. *Dear Lord, please watch out for Ed. Keep him safe.*

She began pacing as the minutes passed, worst-case scenarios racing through her mind. Scenarios where Ed died or disappeared or was seriously hurt. Scenarios where she never found the information, where people kept get-ting hurt.

Finally she saw Ed walking toward her down Main Street. Some of the tension left her shoulders and she rushed to meet him.

She hoped he had news and sometimes hope was the only thing a girl had to hang on to.

* * *

Ed spotted Bailey standing at the end of the street and recognized the concern on her face. She was worried about him, he realized. Something about the thought warmed him.

He hurried toward her.

"Well?" she asked.

"He got away. He had too much of a head start. I don't know how he disappeared, but barring knocking on every door and invading people's privacy, I have no way of finding him."

"What do you say we go talk to a couple of those other workers and see what we can find out?" Bailey asked.

Ed raised his eyebrows, impressed by her deductive reasoning and initiative. "Sounds like a good idea."

They headed for the man who seemed to be giving orders on the dock. The smell of fish and the sound of seagulls defined the area.

He was about to speak when Bailey beat him to it. "Mr. Jeffries, how are you?"

The man, who initially looked gruff, smiled brightly when he spotted Bailey. "It's always good to see you, Bailey."

Bailey knew the man? That was surprising.

"Ed, this is Mr. Jeffries. We go to church together," Bailey explained.

Ed shook his hand, taking in his features. He was probably in his sixties with the thick wrinkles of someone who worked hard outside in the sun. He had white hair, thinning on top, and wore a faded flannel shirt, jeans and work boots.

"That man who was sweeping down here. Do you know much about him?" Bailey asked.

He looked back toward the abandoned broom. "Yeah, that's Arnold. He's new. Just comes in a few days a week."

"How long has he been here?" Ed asked.

"A couple of weeks."

"Know anything else about him?" Ed asked.

"Is he in trouble or something?" Mr. Jeffries crossed his arms, his eyes narrowed with curiosity.

Ed shrugged, trying not to alarm the man. Not yet, at least. "Not trouble, necessarily. We just wanted to ask him some questions."

"I've got to be honest. I didn't do a background check on him. I needed a hand, and he just happened to be there. Seemed like a decent worker. He was quiet, didn't say much."

"Why would he run when he saw us?" Bailey asked.

Mr. Jeffries shrugged. "Beats me. Maybe he's the nervous type. Maybe he has a record and thought you guys were the police. I always noticed that he managed to make himself busy somewhere else every time the sheriff came around, too."

Interesting, Ed thought.

"When's he scheduled to work again?" Ed asked.

"Not until next week."

"Is he staying on the island?" Bailey shielded her eyes against the glare of the sun.

Mr. Jefferies shook his head. "Not that I know of. I'm pretty sure he has a place on the mainland. My impression is that he's desperate for work."

"Thanks, Mr. Jeffries," Bailey said. She squeezed the older gentleman's arm.

"No problem, Bailey. You let me know if you need anything."

"I will, Mr. Jeffries. Thank you."

Bailey and Ed stepped away, headed back toward Main Street.

"You know, it seems like everyone around here is looking out for you."

"Just one more thing to love about island life, right? People do look out for each other."

"I suppose." He looked in the distance, wondering what it would be like to live in a place where he wasn't simply a shadow or he wasn't living a lie, for that matter. It was a luxury he couldn't afford to think about at the moment. "I'm going to go talk to Mary Lou, the housekeeper. You want to come?"

Something flickered in Bailey's gaze. Could it be guilt? Why would Bailey feel guilty, though?

"I would, but I think I'm going to get back to the house and clean up a bit. I've got to earn my keep and all." She shrugged, a little too casually.

He nodded. "All right, then. I'll let you know what she says."

He couldn't help but think that her answer was suspicious. He'd thought that she would jump at the chance to go with him and search for answers. That familiar inkling that she was hiding something returned.

He'd have to address that later. For now, he wanted to talk to his father's old housekeeper, the one who'd up and quit about two weeks before he died.

He walked down the road until he reached a small bungalow. Four tombstones were in the front yard. The island was so small that there was no space for a large cemetery, so many residents buried their loved ones right there on their property. From talking with his dad, Ed knew that Mary Lou's family went back several generations on the island. Her husband had died two decades ago in a boating accident and she'd never remarried.

He knocked at the door. A moment later, a woman with a pouf of bleached-blond hair and oversize tortoiseshell glasses answered. As soon as she saw Ed, she tried to shut the door.

"Wait! I just have a question, Mary Lou."

"I'm not going back to that house," she whispered through the cracked door. "I know who you are. You're Bill Carter's son. You look just like him."

"I'm Ed." He extended his hand.

She stared at his outstretched arm a moment before hesitantly reaching out, half her body still behind the door, and halfheartedly shaking it. "Why are you here?"

"I understand from Bailey that you quit rather suddenly. I just wanted to make sure everything was okay."

"Bailey's a sweet girl. She has a heart of gold for staying around, if you ask me." Her voice left no room for argument.

Ed shifted. "She is sweet, but why did you say it like that?"

Mary Lou pushed her oversize glasses up higher. "Something was going on at the house. I figured I better leave before things got even weirder."

"How were things weird? Please. I'm trying to figure everything out."

Wrinkles formed around her lips as she squeezed them together in thought. Finally, she pulled the door open a little more, but still didn't invite him inside. She stared at him with obvious distrust instead.

"Things kept getting moved." She crossed her arms, as if expecting him to be skeptical.

"What do you mean?"

"I mean, someone was going around the house and touching things. And I'm not talking about Mr. Carter or Bailey. Someone took it upon themselves to go in and out of rooms that no one ever went in. It was like they were playing with my head or something."

"So you quit?"

"Well, because of that and because I kept hearing people walk around at night."

"Really?" Was she crazy? She had a bit of an eccentric vibe to her. Or was someone really messing around in the house?

"No, I'm not crazy." She scowled, as if she'd read his thoughts. "Someone was moving around at night, and again—it wasn't Mr. Carter or Bailey."

"Mary Lou, I'm not doubting you, but how do you know it wasn't one of them?"

"Mr. Carter and Bailey were on the other side of the house. I slept in the west wing. Besides, the footsteps were heavier. Neither Mr. Carter or Bailey weighed that much."

Interesting observation, but it added to her credibility. "Did you tell the police?"

She shook her head. "No, they'd think I was crazy. Besides, Sheriff Davis isn't equipped to find ghosts."

He tried to keep his voice even-keeled. One hint of doubt might make her clam up and never talk to him about this again. "Did you ever consider maybe it was a person? An intruder?"

"Who would break into a house on Smuggler's Cove? No one. This is the safest place around."

That was what most people would think. He wished it was true, but he didn't feel confident. Not anymore.

"Mary Lou, did anything else unusual happen in the days before my father died?"

"Besides the footsteps at night?" She looked in the distance and pursued her lips. "He seemed a bit preoccupied. He disappeared several times."

Ed perked. "What do you mean he disappeared?"

"It was usually when Bailey wasn't around—the times when she'd go into town, for example. He liked to sneak off by himself."

"Any idea what he was doing or where he was going?"

Mary Lou shook her head. "No idea. I figured it wasn't my business and that the man deserved his privacy."

* * *

More than anything, Bailey had wanted to go talk to Mary Lou with Ed. She wanted answers just as much as he did. But she also needed some time alone at the house so she could look for the information her assailant had "requested."

Bailey waited until she was inside the house before she let out the breath she'd been holding. Had Ed suspected anything? Did he have a clue what she was hiding? She prayed he didn't.

Reluctantly, she turned and stared at the living room. Where did she even begin? It wasn't as if she hadn't thought about it before. She'd lain in bed sleepless, wondering where to start.

The problem was searching this whole place would take days. She wasn't even sure there was any information here. But she had to look; she had to do whatever she could.

Mr. Carter had spent most of his time in a smaller living room, set up with a comfy recliner, fireplace and TV, or he'd been in his library or bedroom. Were those places too obvious?

She didn't know but that was where she needed to start.

She glanced out the window and made sure that Ed was nowhere to be seen. He was a bright, perceptive man. Certainly he'd put everything together soon. He'd known that she was up to something—looking for something. That was why she needed to work quickly.

She pushed away her fears about being in this house alone and charged down the hallway. She pushed the door open to the den, as Mr. Carter had called it. The room had dark wood paneling and manly brown leather furniture. A single window allowed some light to flood inside.

Her heart thudded as memories filled her mind. She hadn't been in here since Mr. Carter had passed, and right now grief clutched her heart. The finality of death often gave her pause. While she believed in heaven, it was still hard to comprehend never seeing someone on this earth again.

She shook the thoughts off and rushed toward the recliner. She checked all the crevices there. Nothing.

Next, she checked the bookshelves, under the rug, in the table drawers and everywhere else she could think of.

Nothing.

Of course, she had no idea what she was looking for. She only hoped she'd know it when she saw it.

She glanced one more time at the room but saw nowhere else she could possibly look. Instead, she hurried toward the library. Once there, she quickly glanced out the window, just to make sure that Ed hadn't decided to come back early. She didn't see anyone.

The intruder had already done a good job in this room, tearing everything apart. She had a hard time thinking that there was anything in here, but she had to try. She had to know for sure.

She went through the desk, the bookshelves, the filing cabinets. Almost everything she found was of a business nature. Insurance and car titles and HVAC repair receipts and letters from old friends. Nothing that screamed "the information."

What was she going to do?

She wasn't going to give up. That was what.

She put everything back where she'd found it and then hurried to Mr. Carter's old bedroom. If the information wasn't here, she didn't have any other good ideas on where it could be.

She had no more time to be nostalgic, so instead, she quickly rifled through the drawers, looked between the mattresses, under the rug even. Whatever it was, either she couldn't identify it or it wasn't here.

She paused and put her hands on her hips. What next?

She supposed she would have to search the rest of the house.

But before she could move, she felt a shadow behind her and braced herself for a struggle.

THIRTEEN

Ed stared at Bailey a moment. What was she doing in his father's room?

She twirled around, her fists raised and ready to fight.

Ed caught her before she threw her first punch. He easily overpowered her as he held her hand at bay.

"What are you doing, Bailey?" he demanded.

Her eyes widened before she finally relaxed and lowered her arm. "Ed? What are you doing sneaking up on me like that?"

He let her go, watching carefully to make sure she didn't try to throw any more punches. "I wasn't sneaking up on anyone. It's not my fault if the carpet padded my steps. Besides, I'm not the one who should be answering questions. I want to know what you're doing in my father's room."

He watched her face for a sign of deception. She stared at him a moment, then lines appeared on her forehead and at the corners of her eyes. Her lips pulled downward and her shoulders tensed again.

She was hiding something.

"I was…I was just having a moment. I straightened up the office some, and I was just checking on his room. It's what I do. It's what I've done since I was hired. Do you have a problem with that?"

As much as he wanted to demand the truth from her, Ed knew there were better ways to go about things. Instead, he shook his head. "You've been here more than I have. I appreciate the help."

That seemed to relax her. Some of the fine lines on her face disappeared. "Good. I was hoping you'd feel that way. Old habits are hard to break, you know."

He nodded. Still not buying it. "Mary Lou said she heard footsteps at night."

Bailey froze again. "What?"

Ed nodded and recounted the conversation.

When he was done, Bailey pinched the skin between her eyes. "I never heard anything."

"But you slept in the other wing of the house."

"It just seems like there would be some kind of evidence if someone was coming and going."

Not if they were professionals, Ed thought. This only seemed to confirm that theory. "I just wanted you to know."

"I appreciate it." She glanced at her watch. "It's been a long day. I think I'm going to finish straightening the library and then turn in for the night."

Ed nodded. "Good idea. I have a few phone calls to make anyway. I'll see you in the morning, then."

By the time Bailey finished in the library and reached her room, she felt both exhausted and on edge. That had been close. Too close.

And even though Ed seemed to believe her story, she didn't feel all that confident.

With her bedroom door closed and locked, she walked to the window and pressed her forehead against the cool panes, trying to calm her racing heart. She couldn't live like this. Being deceitful wasn't in her nature. If anything, she was too truthful at times.

"Did you find the information yet?"

Bailey stifled a scream and twirled around at the sound of the deep, unexpected voice. She made out the silhouette of a man sitting in a chair by the window. It had to be the same man who'd threatened her.

She considered running. Or screaming. Or slamming something over his head. Instead, she stayed by the window, her hand reaching for something to use as a weapon. There was nothing. She needed to make it clear to this man that she didn't have the information he'd "requested."

"I don't know where it is or what it is or how to locate it."

He stood and made his way toward her. A mask concealed his features. Bailey shivered, wishing she could disappear.

"You need to find it." His voice sounded low, rumbling, menacing.

"How can I find something when I don't even know what it is?" Her words came out in a rush. "Why don't you get it? You've had the opportunity when we've left the house."

"I can't move about freely."

"Neither can I! Mr. Carter's son is here. He caught me today."

"He can tell you where the information is."

Her heart skipped a beat. What exactly was he implying? "Ed doesn't know. He would have it by now. And if you want the information so badly, why are you trying to kill us?"

"That was just a warning to let you know how serious I am."

"I have no doubt that you're serious." She pressed herself against the wall, wishing she could disappear. "What I don't understand is why you're targeting me. Why not Ed?"

Not that she wanted to put Ed in danger, either. She just needed to keep this man talking. She needed more information.

"The person you need to question is Ed."

"Why?" She gripped the curtain as her pulse spiked in anticipation.

"He's not who he claims to be."

Her throat tightened. "Who is he?"

"Why don't you ask him? Ask him why none of his neighbors know him. Why he has no roots, no past. Where he was when his father died. Ask him."

What was the man talking about? Ed was a DC lawyer who involved himself with cases of international law. He was into the social scene out there. Into getting ahead. Bailey had him all figured...except, what if she didn't? She'd sensed from the beginning there was something else about Ed.

"Your time is running out. I happen to know that your niece has a soccer tournament this weekend. I'd hate for something to happen and ruin her big moment."

"Leave my family out of this." Anger surged in her, making her blood boil.

"Things are going to get ugly and fast. Consider this your last warning."

The man squeezed her neck, some kind of pressure point there, and then everything went black.

Bailey woke up the next morning still lying on the floor.

She sat up, rubbing her neck as everything came back to her.

There'd been a man. In her room. Reminding her of the urgency of the situation.

She stood, her legs wobbly at first. She wandered out of the room, looking for Ed.

He was nowhere. Where did he go? Had the intruder last night hurt him?

She didn't think so. Her intuition was that he'd disappeared on his own and would return soon enough. He was doing the supersecretive thing again and shutting her out. Perhaps proving that his kindness all along had been an act.

Just as she grabbed her coffee, the doorbell rang. It was Todd.

"Mr. Carter's son asked me to come over and look at the window."

"Did he?" Bailey pulled the door open. "By all means, then, come inside."

"So, how's it going?" he asked, walking toward the kitchen with her. "I thought you'd be gone by now."

"I intend on leaving; I'm just helping with a few things around here first." She tried to choose her words carefully. "When did Ed talk to you?"

"He called last night. Said he was going to pick up some supplies today and asked if I could swing by."

"I see."

He set his tools on the table and walked toward the plywood that now covered the window. "I never could believe the rumors I heard about Mr. Carter. He was the talk of the town from the day he moved here."

"What do you mean?" She leaned her hips against the kitchen counter, her interest sufficiently perked.

"I heard he was CIA." His tape measure snapped closed.

Bailey's throat went dry. "What?"

Todd turned to face her. "What? Don't tell me you didn't hear those rumors."

"I didn't, no." Never. Ever. She'd had the inkling he wasn't a number cruncher, but wow.

"Yeah, it's just island scuttlebutt. I know he told everyone he was State Department, but everyone knows that CIA falls under the State Department. People say that's why he was so mysterious and that's why he came here to Smuggler's Cove. What better place for someone with a shady past to retire to? No one would find him here."

Except, what if someone did? What if Ed was right?

"Be safe around that son of his. I don't trust him." Todd raised his chin and pulled his shoulders up.

"Why wouldn't you trust him?" Bailey put her hand on the counter, trying to steady her teetering thoughts.

Todd shook his head, turning back to the window and jotting down some notes. "There's just something about him. He seems too big-city, you know?"

Yeah, Bailey did know. But she'd been beginning to think that Ed was different. She'd started to think her judgment of him was wrong. Maybe she should have trusted her initial impressions.

Maybe she'd been blinded by another corporate-ladder climber again. Though she was in no way interested in him romantically, she needed to remember that most people were out for themselves. To think anything differently, she'd just be fooling herself. For future reference, she needed to remember that all of those guys she read about in her novels were unobtainable. The ones who were loyal, kind and strong only existed in fiction. To dream about them in real life was to set herself up for failure.

"So, what do you think?"

At the sound of Todd's voice, Bailey snapped back to reality. "What?"

"You were in another world there for a second, weren't you? I said, before you head on to a new job, we should get ice cream or something." He closed his notebook and turned to stare at her.

She forced a smile. "Sure. Ice cream is always good."

He grinned. "Great. I'll see you around, then. I got the measurements I needed."

Bailey searched the house again while Ed was gone, but she could still find nothing. She had no idea where that information might be. She looked for papers and files or anything that might trigger a reaction in her. She came up empty. Each time she searched, her despair seemed to grow deeper. How was she ever going to find what that man needed?

She finally gave up and decided to go on a walk. Maybe some fresh air would clear her head. She started down the path, headed toward Samantha's place. She always enjoyed catching up with her friend.

When she cleared the live oak trees, she spotted her friend playing Frisbee on the shoreline with her son. Samantha paused when she saw Bailey and waved her over. "Good to see you! What brings you out this way?"

"Just getting some air."

"Can I get you a drink? Some lemonade maybe?" Connor and his dog, Rusty, took off scurrying down the shoreline, chasing away some seagulls.

Bailey smiled. "I'd love some."

They went inside Samantha's cozy cabin and her friend poured a nice, icy glass of the drink. They sat down at the kitchen table. Outside, John chopped wood.

Samantha leaned toward Bailey, her eyes sparkling. "So…who knew Mr. Carter's son was so hunky?"

Bailey laughed. "You get right to the point, don't you?"

"Why beat around the bush? Is he as nice as he seemed?"

"He's…" What was the word? Bailey shrugged, unsure how to answer. "I'm not certain. Sometimes I think he's unfeeling and other times I think he's everything I assumed he wasn't."

"He sounds quite mysterious, then. Like his father, perhaps?"

Bailey swallowed hard before asking her next question. "Did you hear the rumor that his father was a spy?"

Samantha nodded with hesitation. "Yeah, I heard something like that. You know how people like to make up stories, especially around here. That doesn't mean there's any truth to them."

Bailey had the urge to spill everything, but she knew

she couldn't. Not if there was any possibility that someone was listening. She kept checking her clothes, her watch and her belt for a sign that she'd been bugged. She probably wouldn't recognize a listening device if she saw it, though. That meant she needed to stay quiet.

"Well, I won't tell Todd that he's got some competition." Samantha grinned again.

"Todd and I are just friends." Bailey absently fiddled with the apple-scented candle at the center of the table.

Samantha raised her eyebrows. "You might feel that way, but does he?"

Bailey shrugged. "I have no idea. I haven't tried to lead him on. In all honesty, I'm surprised he's back in town."

"I know. I ran into him a few days ago, right before the storm. He told me his mom is doing much better."

Bailey tensed. "Before the storm?" Certainly Samantha had misspoken.

Samantha nodded. "That's right. We were in town getting some supplies. Why do you look so surprised?'

"Because he told me he just got back yesterday."

Samantha twisted her head in confusion. "Are you sure?"

Bailey nodded. "Yes, I'm positive. For some reason, he lied to me. But why would he do that?"

FOURTEEN

Why would Todd lie to her? The thought wouldn't leave her mind as she walked back to the house. Though she had no interest in dating him, she had a hard time believing he was deceitful. What was he trying to hide?

As Bailey cleared the lane and reached the footbridge leading back to Mr. Carter's estate, she saw something that made her pause. She ducked behind a tree to get a better look.

A tall man with broad shoulders and sunglasses walked from behind the house toward the beach. Bailey's gaze swung in that direction. By the pier, she spotted Ed. He stood with two other men. The three of them huddled together.

What was going on? What if Ed really wasn't trustworthy? Maybe he'd concocted a cover story that would make her heart go out to him, all the while secretly plotting schemes of his own?

Worst yet—what if he really wasn't Mr. Carter's son? After all, his dad always called him Junior, not Ed. He'd never really said his son's real name.

The possibility startled her. But, now that she thought about it, there were no pictures of him anywhere. He'd claimed he had a key that no longer worked, but what if that was a lie? His answers had been vague. He'd said nothing about his father specific enough to prove they were related.

Then again, Mr. Wilkins had recognized him. Certainly that meant that he was the real deal.

Except that old man Wilkins, by all observations, didn't have the best eyesight. He could barely empty the trash and run the riding lawn mower. Bailey had the feeling Mr. Carter had mainly kept him on staff to be kind. He mostly stood in the background, observing the work of others, hiring subcontractors and talking to his boss about fishing and politics. If there was anyone who could be fooled, it would be Mr. Wilkins.

Could one of those men who talked to Ed now be the one who'd sneaked into her room? What if Ed had hired them? What if they were all in this together, some kind of good cop/bad cop routine, and Bailey was the one with the wool pulled over her eyes?

The thought left an unsettled feeling in her stomach.

Bailey stayed behind the tree until the men who'd come with Ed disappeared. They rode away in one boat and left another. She watched as Ed made his way toward the house. His gaze swung around as he walked across the lawn, almost as if he could feel that he was being watched.

Once he disappeared inside, Bailey finally pushed herself away from the tree. It was time to find out exactly where Ed had been all day and, with any luck, who exactly he was.

Ed was pulling a glass from the cabinet in the kitchen when Bailey walked inside, her cheeks red with exertion. His pleasure at seeing her surprised him.

But that pleasure quickly disappeared when he saw the fire in her eyes.

"What are you up to?" she demanded, a hand on her hip.

"Excuse me?" What in the world was she talking about? He filled his glass with water from the tap, sure to keep his actions easy and natural. He'd had years of practice.

Christy Barritt   133

She stepped closer. "Who were those men with you out there on the pier? What are you planning?"

His back muscles tightened. So Bailey had seen him out there. He'd hoped to keep it quiet and on the down low. He should have known better.

"Oh, that. I had to go into town to pick up something." He took a long sip, both because he was parched and to give her time to work out her thoughts. He could learn a lot about her through her accusations.

She leaned toward him, indignation in her gaze. "Who are you, Ed? Are you really Mr. Carter's son?"

She was thinking like a spy now. Kudos to her.

He set his empty glass on the counter with a thud. "Of course I'm Mr. Carter's son. Why would you ask that?"

"Because something's not adding up, and I don't like being deceived."

"Why do you think I'm deceiving you?"

"For starters, how do I know that you're really his son? There are no pictures. He only called his son Junior. Your key didn't work. Why don't you start talking, because I'd really like to hear what you have to say?"

"How can I prove that to you?" He kept his voice easy, calm.

"What was your father's favorite football team?"

"Redskins."

She shook her head. "Everyone from DC says that. Favorite hobby?"

"Fishing."

She squeezed the skin between her eyes. "Of course that would be a logical guess since he moved to a fishing village." She lowered her hand, determination in her gaze. "What was his wife's name?"

Ed stepped closer. "My mom was Theresa. She was the CEO of a nonprofit and she died in a car accident when I was in college. My dad had a certain amount of security clearance through his job, so he liked to keep his family life private. My father was an only child. His right index finger was cut off at the knuckle because of a hunting accident when he was seventeen, and he liked to put protein powder in his coffee."

He saw the mix of relief, confusion and exhaustion on her face, and he stepped closer. "I am his son, Bailey. We have the same eyes. That's what everyone has always said."

She frowned. "I guess I believe you. I just don't know who to trust anymore. One minute, I think you're different from other guys—in a good way. The next minute, I feel convinced that you're hiding something and aren't who you claim to be."

He squeezed her arm, trying to figure out the best way to smooth over a bumpy situation. He wanted more than anything to put her at ease, to reassure her. But he couldn't do that. He couldn't promise that he wasn't like the other guys who'd broken her heart. He had too much baggage, too many secrets he couldn't speak of. Not now. Maybe not ever.

But there was one thing he was certain of. "Bailey, you can trust me."

Her gaze softened, but only for a moment before she raised her chin defiantly. "How can I be sure of that?"

"You have to take my word for it." He wanted to give her more. He really did. But his hands were tied.

"That's all you can offer me?"

He felt his defenses coming down when he heard the earnestness in her voice. "There are things I can't tell you, Bailey. But I'm on your side. We're both on the same side. The side of justice."

Her hands went to her hips. "Is what they say true?"

He released her arm and leaned against the counter, trying to take hold of his thoughts. "Depends on what you're talking about."

"Was your father a spy?"

He let out a tense chuckle, hoping she didn't hear any truth in the sound. "My dad? A spy? Where did you hear that?"

"You're not answering the question."

Bailey could see through him and that fact left him feeling unnerved. He found his water glass and refilled it. "My dad was not a spy."

She stared at him, unsure what to say or think.

"You can trust me, Bailey," he repeated. He meant it. Aside from the secrets he'd been sworn not to share, Bailey could depend on him. He vowed not to let her down. "I would tell you more if I could."

"What *can* you tell me?"

He reached into his pocket and pulled out a paper. "I can tell you that the lab found traces of arsenic in my father's heart medicine."

Bailey gasped, taking the paper from him. "No…"

He nodded, feeling somber as he confirmed what he'd thought all along. "It's true. Someone tampered with his prescription. My father was murdered, Bailey. This confirms it. No more doubts."

"But why?" Her voice sounded strained, subdued.

He motioned outside. "Let's take a walk."

She nodded, looking dazed. He put a hand on her elbow and led her outside. He wasn't sure why he felt the urge to get out of the house, but he did. The whole place could feel stifling with too many reminders of his father's passing. Then there were the cameras he'd found. What if the whole place was bugged?

They walked silently until they reached the beach. Ed zipped his jacket up, the wind chilly coming off the water. Bailey shoved her hands into the pockets of her sweatshirt.

"Bailey, my dad had a high-level position with the State Department. He made a lot of enemies."

"Enemies who might have wanted him dead?"

"Plenty, I'm sure."

"There's no one who can help us?"

He shook his head. "I've seen too much, Bailey."

"A lawyer who's seen too much, huh?" Her voice lilted.

He wanted to pour everything out to her. He wanted to trust her and for her to trust him. But there were certain constraints that he had no control over. He had to change the subject.

"Why aren't you married yet, Bailey? You seem like the marrying type." At least, that was how Ed saw her. She was the type of woman a man wanted to come home to—kind, pretty, compassionate and warm. For some reason, she'd ended up here at this isolated island, where her chances were slim to none as far as finding anyone to share her life with.

"That ex-boyfriend I told you about? We were actually engaged."

"What happened?"

"We had the wedding set and everything." She shook her head. "I know this is going to sound strange, but he wanted to reschedule the date of our wedding to better accommodate his work schedule."

"Really?" Ed could only imagine how that had gone over.

She nodded. "Yeah, really. He was an ad executive, and he had big plans for the future. For *his* future, that is. I'd felt like second place to his job nearly since the beginning of our relationship. But I think that was the final straw. I saw the rest of my life with him, and it wasn't happy. It wasn't what I wanted for my future."

"I understand."

"I'm really not the jealous type who wants someone to dote over me. But I do want someone who has priorities, who knows how to separate work from his personal life. I want someone who realizes there's more to life than bringing in a big paycheck. Having time with loved ones is more important than getting ahead at work."

"I agree. Those are wise words." His attraction to Bailey continued to grow, as if it were out of his control. "You really do like it here on Smuggler's Cove, don't you?"

She nodded. "I do. Maybe I need to get with modern times, but I like feeling like I've stepped into another era—an era from the past."

"You're different, Bailey. And that's a good thing."

She stole a glance at him. "Enough about me. How about you? Have you dated any since that girl broke your heart?"

He glanced up in surprise. He'd forgotten that he had told her about his engagement. "Claire? No, I can't say I have."

"And what happened with Claire that made you leery of dating?"

"Claire wasn't who I thought she was. When she was with me, she pretended to be one person. When we weren't together, she was someone else entirely. When I realized that, I felt disillusioned and deceived. I didn't like it. I haven't dated, nor have I had the desire to date since that."

"Understood."

Good. He needed to put that boundary in place. Because he knew his feelings for Bailey were growing, and it was best to squash any potential relationship before it started.

No matter how hard that choice might be.

There was something about the thought of Ed being hurt that caused a surge of protectiveness to rise in Bailey.

The fact that he'd opened up about his hurt made Bailey somehow feel more connected to him. He wasn't just the tough, slick cardboard figure of a man. He had a past; he had a history.

There were still a lot of blanks that needed to be filled in, though.

Every time her doubts started to cloud her judgment, Ed surprised her by opening up and showing a different side of himself. Put all of that together, and she felt like a tangled mess of emotions.

Bailey shoved her hands deeper into her pockets and enjoyed the feeling of the breeze hitting her face. Something about the two of them walking side by side, even without saying a word, felt right. The mere thought went against every part of her instincts.

She didn't want to trust again; didn't want to be hurt again. But Ed Carter was intriguing. And, when he let that side of him show through, he was kind.

"Ed, have you looked in the barn yet?"

"Did my dad ever go out there?"

Bailey shrugged. "He liked having moments by himself, just like I did, I guess. I usually went up to the widow's walk. He really liked the library, but he did come out to the garage and visit Mr. Wilkins some."

"It's worth a shot."

They started together across the yard. Ed unlocked the door leading to the garage, a building that was larger than some people's homes. The shop area waited on the other side. This was where most of the tools and equipment were kept. Though Mr. Carter wasn't the handy type himself, the previous owners had been. This had been a nice little workshop for someone at one time. The old equipment was still here, showing evidence of a true artisan. The scent of sawdust and oil saturated the space.

"I wouldn't mind using some of this one day," Ed muttered.

Bailey looked up at him in surprise. "Really?"

He leaned down to examine a machine. "Yeah, really.

I've always enjoyed working with my hands. I liked building bookshelves and footstools when I was in high school."

"That surprises me. I see you more as the playing-football type."

"I did that, too. But we moved a lot. My dad was gone a lot. I had these visions of building my own boat one day and sailing across the bay—maybe even the ocean. Anyway, working with my hands always helps me to feel relaxed."

"It's important to find something you can do to help you unwind."

He ran his hand down one of the tools. "Funny, I actually haven't thought about that in a long time."

"Well, maybe you can now. This place is yours. It will be the perfect place for you to come on weekends or whenever you need to get away."

His lips pulled into a tight line. "You never know. Maybe I'll do that."

Bailey sighed and glanced around. "I'm not even sure what we're looking for exactly."

"Yeah, me neither."

They searched the cabinets and under things and between old pieces of wood. There was nothing.

"There's also the barn area," Bailey reminded him.

"It's worth a look."

They stepped through a door and, even though there hadn't been animals in this space for probably a decade, the smell seemed to be a part of the building. Bailey absorbed the odor of hay and dank earth and the musky scent of fading sunlight.

"This makes me want to grab a good book and a blanket and curl up in the hay with it," Bailey murmured.

Ed looked over at her and smiled, an unidentifiable emotion in his gaze.

"What? What was that look for?" Bailey asked.

"Nothing."

"It was most definitely something." She raised an eyebrow.

"I just like the way you think, Bailey. I can't see myself curling up with a book, but curling up in the hay sounds nice."

"Curling up in the hay by yourself sounds nice?" she asked.

He let out a quick laugh. "Let's just keep looking."

Bailey didn't ask any more questions.

They searched each of the stalls, under the hay, between slats in the wood. Nothing.

Ed nodded up toward the ceiling. "Hayloft. Last place, other than the actual garage. I'm not sure my dad could have gotten up there, though."

"He was rather sprightly up until the last couple of weeks. I mean, sure, he had episodes before that. But he didn't want to slow down."

"Sounds like my dad. Maybe I should check it out first, just in case it's rickety."

"No way. I'm going, too."

"Enter at your own risk."

"You know it."

Ed climbed the wooden ladder first, but Bailey stayed on his heels. Once Ed reached the top, he stretched his hand out to help her up. Bailey flinched at the electricity that shot through them as their hands connected.

As soon as she could, she pulled her hand away and wiped her palm on her jeans. That spark had been unexpected, and she didn't know what to do about the fact that her heart was suddenly pounding out of control.

Ed seemed unaffected and coolly in charge of all of his emotions still. The feeling had been one-sided, and that was fine with Bailey. She wasn't looking for fireworks.

Just to save her sister's life. And a job would be nice, once all this chaos was over.

Unfortunately the blast of electricity left her feeling unbalanced. She took a step away from the ladder, only to trip on something. Ed caught her arm, but that only diffused her fall. She hit the hay and a whiff of dust ballooned into her face, making her sneeze.

"You okay?" Ed asked, bending down beside her.

She pushed herself up and sneezed. "Yeah, just fine."

"I told you it might be rickety here."

She scowled. "Yes, you did."

"Why don't you stay here while I check the rest of this place out?"

She flipped over, off her stomach and into sitting position. She hated to admit it, but he was right. "Sure."

The loft was surprisingly large and, though she'd pictured only hay bales, there were several things that were covered up. She watched as Ed moved the sheet off the first mystery item. There were old bags of fertilizer. He searched between them and then put the sheet back over the stash.

As he was walking toward the next sheet-covered mass, the floor suddenly gave way. Ed went tumbling downward.

FIFTEEN

Bailey screamed as she leaped to her feet and ran across the loft toward Ed. She slowed her steps as she got closer, fearing more of the floor would give out. But before she even reached Ed, he'd pulled himself out and sat against the wall. Hay sprinkled his hair.

"Told you it wasn't safe," he muttered.

Something about the way he said the words caused Bailey to chuckle. Her chuckle turned into a full-out laugh, and Ed joined her. They sat there, both covered in hay and sneezing, and for probably no reason.

"I feel like we're two kids who've snuck up here without our parents' permission," Bailey said, throwing a piece of straw from her hair to the floor.

"Tell me about it. I can't imagine my father coming up here, not at his age. We obviously can't even handle it."

Bailey let out another long chuckle, the action a nice break from the tension.

Ed pushed himself up. "Let me check out these other two things, and then let's get down."

Bailey swiped the ground with her hands and froze at what she saw. "Ed. Look at this."

He carefully crossed the floor toward her and bent down. There was fresh, new wood underneath the hay. A section of this loft had been replaced.

Ed continued to wipe away the hay, and what almost

seemed like a walkway right down the center emerged. "How did we miss this?" he muttered.

"I think it's right over the rafters. Listen." Bailey knocked on the wood. The sound was dull and without any echo or reverberation.

Ed smiled. "I believe you're right. That would be the most secure part of the floor anyway. It makes sense."

The walkway led to a covered object against the far wall. Bailey followed Ed, making sure to stay on the new section of planks. She held her breath when they reached the end. Ed glanced at her before pulling the sheet down.

What they saw there surprised them both.

Ed blinked at what was beneath the sheet. He'd expected more farm equipment. Maybe a filing cabinet, at best. Instead, he saw—

"Lab equipment? What in the world is this?" Bailey asked.

Ed shook his head. "I have no idea why this is here."

He stared at the worktable. There was a microscope, some camera negatives, cellophane and developing fluid.

"Maybe your dad took up photography and didn't tell anyone?" Bailey offered.

Ed shook his head. "I wish there was a simple, logical explanation. That's highly unlikely."

"If not photography, what was he doing with this?"

"I have no idea."

Ed lifted things off the table, looking for a picture, a paper, a camera. There was nothing.

Of course his dad had covered his tracks. His dad was the best at what he did, and Ed wouldn't expect anything less. But that didn't help Ed find any answers. What exactly had his dad been up to?

"What are we going to do now?" Bailey asked.

"We?" Certainly Ed hadn't heard the question correctly.

Bailey nodded. "I'm in this with you. If someone hurt your father, then I failed in my job as his nurse. I was supposed to watch out for him."

His heart slowed to a thud. "No one could have known."

"Still, I feel responsible. I just don't understand how someone switched the medication."

"Whoever did it was good. Whatever that information was that Elmer Martin brought to him, I have a feeling someone wants to get his or her hands on it. It's either because whatever's in those files is incriminating or because it contains highly sensitive information that's capable of bringing down organizations. Countries for that matter."

Bailey shook her head and stepped closer, glancing over all the equipment. She finally paused. "I don't know what to say about all of this. I never remember your dad talking about photography. The only hobby I remember your dad talking about—besides fishing and golfing—was listening to his old James Taylor albums."

Ed glanced at her. "James Taylor? My dad didn't like James Taylor."

"He talked about him…"

"What?" Ed asked.

Bailey nodded, unwavering. "He mentioned him before he died. I figured he was talking about the singer/songwriter." Bailey shook her head. "Is there someone else named James Taylor, Ed? Was that some kind of clue that I didn't even pick up on?"

"It's worth looking into. In fact, let's get back to the house and do that now. In the meantime, I'm going to give some more thought to this equipment and ask Wilkins about this walkway."

"I doubt he could get up here to build this."

Ed agreed. "But Todd could have."

"It looks like maybe we're getting some leads."

"Yes, *we* are." Bailey grinned.

Somehow, being in this together didn't feel so bad at the moment. He only hoped Bailey didn't get hurt in the process. He would do everything within his power to ensure that didn't happen.

The next morning, Bailey pulled her jacket closer as the wind whipped over the boat. When Ed had returned yesterday morning from the mainland, he'd brought his boat with him, which allowed them the freedom to come and go as they pleased.

Today, they were going to meet with Mr. Carter's lawyer to hear the last will and testament being read. A knot of apprehension had formed in Bailey's stomach at the thought. She really didn't want anything to do with Mr. Carter's estate, but since he'd requested that she be there, she'd honor his wishes.

After they finished with that meeting, they planned to pay a surprise visit to James Taylor. Ed had called someone last night and had volunteered a limited amount of information to Bailey. Apparently, there was a man with that name affiliated with Mr. Carter through the State Department. He was now retired and living in a DC suburb. Nothing about him seemed suspicious.

Maybe—just maybe—he would have some answers for them. They so desperately needed answers right now, and each of their leads so far had seemed to fizzle out.

When they reached the mainland, the rental car Ed had arranged for them was waiting at the pier. Bailey watched carefully as Ed inspected the vehicle as though he was suspicious something might be wrong with it. It didn't do much to help Bailey relax on the drive. Had he been looking for a car bomb? A bug? She didn't ask; she figured it was better not to know and that Ed wouldn't tell her anyway.

"You know this lawyer?" Bailey asked. "A.J. Andrews?"

Ed shook his head. "Nope. Never met him, never heard of him."

"Ed, I just want you to know that even if something was left to me by your father, I'm not going to take it. I don't do this job so people can leave me things after they die. I'm going to the meeting just out of respect for your father."

"I know you're not a gold digger, Bailey. If my father wanted you to have something, you should take it. My father never made halfhearted decisions. If he left you something, it was for a reason."

"I appreciate the vote of confidence, but I'm still not sure I'm comfortable taking anything." She was just ready to get this meeting over with.

A few minutes later, they pulled to up a regal-looking redbrick building in downtown Richmond. Ed found a parking space on the street before they hurried up the steps and through the heavy wooden doors at the front of the building.

"Ed Carter. We've been expecting you." The receptionist turned to Bailey. "And you must be Bailey. We're glad you both could make it."

Bailey and Ed exchanged a glance. Did every client get this greeting?

"Come with me," the receptionist continued.

They followed the woman across lush carpet, down the hall and to the office at the end. A man sat behind a desk there. He was younger than what Bailey had expected— probably in his midthirties. He had dark hair, appeared tall, and…he had a cleft in his chin.

"You're the man who stopped by to see me at Mr. Carter's house," Bailey mumbled. He fit the description Mr. Wilkins had given her perfectly.

The man didn't flinch. "That was me."

"Why'd you go to Smuggler's Cove?" Bailey refused to move from the doorway, not until the man explained himself.

"Why don't you sit down and I'd be happy to clarify." He pointed to the leather chairs in front of him.

Bailey shook her head. "I'd rather you expound first."

His wide, bright smile dimmed. "I was coming to check you out." He laced his hands together on the desk. "I counted Mr. Carter as a friend, and I didn't want to see him make a mistake."

"You wanted to make sure I was trustworthy, in other words."

"In so many words, I suppose the answer would be yes. Last-minute changes to a person's will can raise red flags," A.J. explained.

"When exactly did my father make changes to his will?" Ed asked, his eyebrows knit together.

"About a month before he died. I believe you brought him over here on the ferry, Bailey, and he said he had some errands he wanted to do on his own."

Bailey nodded. "That's right. I went into town to do some shopping and take care of my own business."

"Mr. Carter was here meeting with me." He pointed to the seats again. "Now, I think you'd be more comfortable if you sat, but we can do this your way."

Ed led Bailey to a seat, and they both made themselves comfortable. Bailey's mind was racing, though. Thank goodness Ed was with her now because she needed his wisdom. Quite possibly his protection, too, if she were to be honest.

"All right." The lawyer pulled out a file and opened it. "I won't keep you in suspense any longer."

Ed's mind raced as they left the attorney's office. There was something he didn't quite trust about A.J. Andrews.

He'd expected his dad to hire someone older, with more experience. Why had his father hired that man, of all people? Was his reputation so glowing that he'd overlooked the man's age? Was this man connected in some way with the CIA?

Neither he nor Bailey said anything after the meeting, except mentioning lunch. They found a deli down the street, ordered sandwiches and then found a corner booth to eat.

"What do you think?" Bailey asked. She took a long sip of her iced tea.

Ed shook his head. "I don't know what to think. Something seems a little suspicious about all of this."

"You think your father was trying to send a message through his will?"

Ed shook his head again, trying to let everything set in. His father had left him the entire estate, with the stipulation that Ed not sell the property. He'd left Bailey access to the widow's walk whenever she wanted, as well as the golf cart and his collection of books.

Access to the widow's walk? What an odd bequest. If Ed owned the property, that essentially gave Bailey permission to use his property whenever she wanted.

"I don't expect to use the widow's walk whenever I want," Bailey offered, wiping her mouth.

"I'm not opposed to you using it. The bequest was just strange, wouldn't you say? Not at all like my father."

Bailey nodded. "Especially if you do settle down there one day. I certainly wouldn't want to interrupt your time so I could use the upstairs—what's rightfully mine." She smiled, but her lips quickly flattened into a frown. "I don't know what to say. I never thought of your dad as eccentric, but..."

"My dad always did things on purpose. These things weren't haphazard. He had his reasons—I just don't know what they are."

The will had also mentioned something about letters he'd left for both Bailey and Ed that better explained his decisions. What he hadn't said was where these letters were, and Ed had to wonder why he hadn't just left them with his attorney.

"Do you think the break-in at the office is connected with all of this?" Bailey asked.

Ed bit down. Before they'd left, A.J. had said that someone had broken in three nights ago. Nothing had been taken, but the police hadn't caught the person behind it, either. Whoever had broken in had tried to get to the attorney's files, but had been unable to breach the locks.

"It very well could be," Ed said. "Nothing would really surprise me at this point."

And Ed still couldn't wrap his mind around the equipment he'd found in the hayloft. The answers weren't coming together nearly as quickly as he'd hoped. He almost thought his dad…was hinting that Ed and Bailey should be together. What other reason would he have to grant her unlimited access to the house? It was the only thing that made sense.

Had his father known something that Ed hadn't? Had he seen something in Bailey that he thought would be good for Ed?

With every new answer he uncovered, the more tangled this web seemed to get. In the back of his mind, he wondered about Sanderson, as well. Was he involved with any part of this scheme? Had he discovered Ed's real identity and decided to come after him?

Ed was going to look into this attorney. Then he had to figure out how to honor his father's wishes while preserving national security.

"Any idea what we'll say to this James Taylor when we get there?" Bailey asked as they cruised down the road after lunch.

"Just let me do the talking. Follow my lead."

She nodded, any hope she had of Ed just being a lawyer crumbling the more she got to know him. She had a feeling he was following in his father's footsteps. Did he also work for the State Department? Maybe. But there was more to his story.

They drove two hours up toward DC and finally pulled up to a country-style home located on several acres of property in the remote suburbs. The homes in this area were more than nice. They were luxurious and affluent.

"Stay close," Ed cautioned as they got out of the car.

They approached the sweeping porch—Ed first—and rang the doorbell. Bailey observed the potted plants, the stained-glass window by the entryway, the cheerful welcome mat. At least the house *seemed* warm and welcoming.

Bailey's anticipation deepened. Would this man have any answers? Was that asking too much?

After several minutes passed, it became apparent that no one was coming to greet them.

"Should we head back?" Bailey asked.

Ed's eyes narrowed with the thought. "Not yet."

He started down the steps and began to skirt around the house. He peered into the garage window. "His car is here."

"Maybe he has more than one," Bailey suggested.

Ed shook his head in that way that made her think he knew something she didn't. "I think someone's home."

"Why would you say that?"

"Because I can still smell the bacon they cooked for breakfast."

Bailey's chills intensified. What was going on? Were they too late getting here? Had something happened to James Taylor?

Before she could ask any more questions, a bullet whizzed past. Ed threw her on the ground just as another one buzzed by her ear.

Someone was shooting at them.

Which meant they were onto something.

She only hoped they lived long enough to pursue their new lead.

"Who's trying to kill us?" Bailey yelled.

Ed pushed her head back down, sheltering her from the incoming bullets. "I don't know. Stay down, though."

He reached into his jacket and pulled out his gun. He should have never brought Bailey with him. Of course, who would have known this would happen?

"We need to get you back to the car."

"What about you?" Bailey asked, panic lacing her voice.

"I'll worry about me."

"Is there just one shooter?" She pressed her face into the house, almost as if she was trying to become one with the wall there.

He lifted his head, trying to get a glimpse of something—anything. It was no use. "As far as I can tell, the bullet came from the garage."

Just then, more ammunition hit the ground.

"Stay where you are," Ed ordered.

He raised his gun and peered around the corner. He couldn't see anything. He had to get closer.

He crept toward the garage, staying low. Cautious. On guard.

He counted to three and dived toward a gazebo between the garage and the house. More bullets flew, barely missing him.

When things went still, Ed peered up. Someone peeked around the window. He'd only seen part of the face, but the man looked familiar.

Was that...? Could it be...?

"James? James Taylor?" Ed spoke loudly, trying to make sure his voice carried. "It's me. Ed Carter. Bill's son. We just want to talk."

Silence stretched, tight and thick. Finally, a man stepped out, still holding his gun, his face scrunched with distrust.

James stared at him a moment before lowering his gun and nodding. "You have the same eyes."

"That's what people always say."

James scanned behind them. "You may not be safe here. We should get inside."

"What's going on?" Ed didn't like the implications of what he was saying.

"I'll tell you once you're inside. But I can't promise my house will be safe for much longer." He waved him toward the house.

Ed reached for Bailey and kept her close as James ushered them inside. He quickly closed the door, turned three locks into place and pulled a safety latch shut. He wasn't taking any chances.

"Let's go in the den," James ordered. "There are no windows there."

They stepped into a dark room, located off the main entry. Deer heads, ducks, hunting caps and guns decorated the walls.

Every part of Ed was on alert, waiting for what would happen next. He knew the gut-wrenching feeling of when danger lurked close by and that was what he felt now.

James stood by the entryway, the pistol still in his hands. His gaze was tense, constantly scanning the rest of the house, as if he suspected someone might come bursting inside at any minute.

"What's going on, James?" Ed asked, standing on the other side of the doorway.

He nodded warily at Bailey. "Who's that?"

"I'm Bailey. I was Bill Carter's nurse."

"Can you trust her?" James looked at Ed.

Ed nodded. "Yeah, we can trust her."

James peered around the corner again. "Someone's after me. I'm sure of it."

"Why are you so sure?" Ed asked.

"Elmer Martin stopped by about two weeks ago. He had some papers."

Finally! Maybe they'd get some answers.

"Papers worth killing over?" Ed asked.

James scanned the front of his house again. "Absolutely worth killing for. I told him he needed to turn the information over to the authorities. He told me he couldn't."

"Why?"

"He thought some of the higher-ups were working for the other side. He didn't know whom he could trust. Then I heard he ended up dead. Not long after that, I started getting that feeling like someone was watching me. I knew your father's death wasn't from natural causes. I also know my turn is coming up soon."

"How'd you know my dad?" Ed asking, trying to gauge the man's level of truth.

"We worked together at the State Department. I retired a few years before he did."

"What did this information pertain to?" Ed asked.

"It's twofold. It implicates people at the CIA, but it also reveals intel about the hostage—"

Just then, glass at the front of the house shattered.

SIXTEEN

"It's a grenade!" Ed shouted. "Get down!"

Ed covered Bailey with his body just as an explosion rocked the house. Debris rained down on them. When the flames ceased, smoke lingered in the air.

Bailey waited to hear the sounds of men invading the house. Of gunfire. Of more grenades.

Instead, she heard the sizzle of fire and the crackling flames in the aftermath of the explosion.

Ed pushed himself off Bailey and glanced back. James lay on the floor, a section of the wall on top of him. Ed scrambled toward the man and put a finger at his neck.

"He's dead," he muttered. "The blast got him."

"What are we going to do?" Panic threatened to overtake her, but she held the emotion at bay. She'd never survive this if she succumbed to her fears. Despite her attempted bravado, trembles shook her muscles.

"We've got to get out of here. Stay where you are while I find a way out."

She grabbed Ed's arm, the thought of being alone—or something happening to Ed—enough to shake her to the core. "Let me go with you."

He leaned closer, his chest heaving with exertion and adrenaline. He squeezed her arm, locking his eyes with hers. "It's safer here."

"I don't care. Please don't leave me alone."

He finally nodded and motioned for her to stay close. Bailey kept one hand gripping his arm as they crept toward the entryway. Ed stayed against the wall, moving slowly, stealthily. He reached the window and peered around.

"What do you see?"

"Nothing," he whispered, his muscles taut beneath her hand. "Absolutely nothing."

Bailey wasn't sure if that was good or bad.

"I don't know what they're planning," Ed muttered. "We need to get out of here, though."

"Just how do you plan on doing that?"

He hurried back toward James, reached into his pocket and pulled out his keys. "I have an idea."

Bailey stayed behind him as he rushed through the house. Ed slowly opened a door near the kitchen. Darkness stared at them from the other side. Carefully, Ed took his first step inside the room.

The garage, Bailey realized. This was the garage.

Ed reached for her hand and pulled her inside the room. The silence was almost scarier than the bullets had been.

Bailey waited for someone to jump out, for someone to attack. Nothing happened. The only sound was that of their feet on the cement beneath them.

Quietly, Ed unlocked the passenger door of the massive black SUV parked there. He ushered her inside and gently closed the door with barely a click.

Bailey's skin crawled as she anticipated what might happen next. Would they be ambushed? Were these bad guys just waiting for Ed's next move, just waiting for another attack? She didn't know, and not knowing had caused her blood pressure to spike uncontrollably.

Ed silently climbed inside.

"Put your seat belt on," he whispered.

With trembling fingers, she fastened it in place. She had no choice at the moment but to trust Ed completely.

Quickly, he slipped the keys into the ignition. Then he cranked the engine, put the car in Drive and jammed his foot on the gas. The vehicle burst through the garage door.

Bailey screamed. Her fingers dug into the leather upholstery of the seat as the momentum of the car jolted her.

They sped past Ed's rental car as bullets began flying through the air. Their assailants must have been hiding in the woods because no one was visible. But the danger was all too real.

Ed drove full speed until they reached the busy metro area. "I don't think anyone followed us."

Bailey said nothing, only stared at the street, partly terrified, partly in shock.

"You okay?" he asked, squeezing her knee.

She nodded, trying to pry her fingers from the seat and willing her breathing to return to normal. "Yeah, I'm fine. I think."

"It appears we lost them."

"Who are they?" Bailey asked, hardly hearing anything above the pounding in her ears.

"Someone who wants that information."

"If they wanted it so badly, wouldn't they have kept James alive so they could find it?" Bailey's voice sounded squeaky and high, even to her own ears.

"My guess is that once these guys realize James knew what those files said, his name went on a hit list."

Bailey's throat went dry enough that she rubbed the tight muscles at her neck, willing herself to gulp in deep breaths. "So, you think anyone who knows what's in those files will ultimately die?"

Ed stared at the road ahead, dodging in and out of traffic. "That's my guess. Someone doesn't want anyone to know what's in those files. They're trying to stop the information from being spread."

"What's so important?"

"Matters of national security. Guilty parties. Ruined reputations of countries. Uncovering the names of spies. It could be any number of things."

"None of that is comforting." Once she found the information, these guys were going to kill her, she realized. There was no happy ending in all of this for her, no matter what she did. "James said something about a hostage. What was he talking about?"

"I have no idea. Not yet." Ed glanced over at her. "Why do you look like you're going to pass out?"

She fanned her face for a moment. "I'm just feeling a little overwhelmed."

He reached across the seat and grabbed her hand. "I'll watch out for you, Bailey."

His touch was surprisingly comforting and brought her a measure of peace she hadn't expected. She squeezed his hand in appreciation. "Thank you. I'm not sure that's going to be possible, though."

"What's going on, Bailey? Is there anything you need to tell me?"

She wanted to spill everything. After all, what were the chances that man would overhear any of the conversation here?

But she'd seen what those men could do. They would kill her sister without thinking twice about it. The man's threat hadn't been empty.

So, as much as she'd like to pour everything out to Ed right here, she couldn't. She had to figure a way out of this mess on her own.

"I'm just trying to sort everything out," she whispered.

Ed retracted his hand, and she instantly missed the warmth. Instead, he put both hands on the steering wheel as he maneuvered the vehicle through traffic.

"I'm trained to tell when a person's lying, Bailey," he muttered.

His words caused the blood to drain from her face. "I'm not trained, but I can also tell when someone's not telling the truth. Maybe you should point that finger back at yourself." She hated to sound harsh, but she wasn't the only one hiding things. He was no DC lawyer. Or, if he was, there was more to the story.

Silence stretched between them for the rest of the ride.

Bailey tried to tell herself that she didn't care, but she knew that deep down inside, she did. Against all the odds, she was beginning to care about Ed Carter, the last person she wanted to have feelings for.

"This isn't the way back to the boat ramp," Bailey muttered.

She was as observant as always. Of course, he already knew the woman was smart. She was putting things together a little too easily. "There's one more person I'd like to talk to, Bailey. Plus, it's getting late. I don't want to be on the water at night."

"Don't I get a say in this? What does that mean for tonight?"

"We'll find a hotel. I think it would be for the best, especially after what happened earlier."

He could tell by the tight line of her lips that she was uncomfortable, suspicious and scared.

He wanted to grab her hand again, but knew it was a bad idea on more than one level. "Bailey, you're just going to have to trust me. I know it's not easy. But, believe me, I wouldn't do anything to hurt you."

She looked toward him, her cheeks flushing. "I hope you're right."

Something about being around her caused a surge of protectiveness to rise in him. He knew he'd do whatever it took to keep her safe. He also knew he was entering dangerous territory. It had been a long time since he'd felt anything for a woman. Physical danger, plus having his heart involved, was never a good mix.

He reminded himself to keep his distance.

"Who's this other person we're going to talk to?" Bailey asked. Her voice sounded strained.

"An old friend. He's very wise. Should have some good insight for us."

"Can you trust him?"

"I think so."

"You don't sound so sure." She scrutinized him.

"Nothing's ever sure in my world, Bailey. Except God."

"God's a great place to start. The only place really."

Ed nodded. "That's the truth."

It was so refreshing to be with someone who understood and shared his beliefs. He was finding it less common, and he was more often an outsider when it came to his spiritual beliefs. It felt good to be around someone who was like-minded.

The rest of the ride was silent. He couldn't help but wonder about what James had said. He'd mentioned a hostage. Could he have been talking about the Reginald Peterson ordeal? Reginald was an American contractor who'd been taken hostage by the Kurdistan government. People had suspicions that Sanderson was involved. There was obviously more to this story.

Finally, they pulled up to an apartment complex in Alexandria. The area was clean, neat and expensive.

Skipping the elevator, they took the stairs to the third floor. Ed knocked on the door, his gaze constantly searching the surrounding area. A man with spiked light brown hair and a thin, lean build answered. He didn't smile, didn't reach out for a warm handshake, didn't offer any formalities.

"This is my old friend Micah Stephens," Ed said, turning toward Bailey.

Micah briefly nodded before scanning behind them. "Were you followed?"

Ed shook his head. "No, we weren't."

"Come on inside. I wondered when you'd show up. I just got in from out of town. Your timing is good."

Ed put his hand on Bailey's back and ushered her inside first. He didn't like where all of this was going. Not for a moment.

Now Bailey was in the crosshairs, as well.

Once the door was securely locked, Ed turned toward Bailey. "Would you mind if I talked to Micah alone?"

Fire lit in her eyes. "As a matter of fact, I would. I'm just as much in danger as anyone else. I think I deserve to know what's going on."

Micah and Ed exchanged a glance. Finally, Ed nodded, praying that his gut was right. "You can trust her."

"Clearance?"

Ed shook his head. "But she's got a lot at stake in this."

Micah nodded. "Okay, then. Sit down. We've got a lot to talk about."

Bailey felt anticipation building inside her. Whatever was going on, it was big. She prayed she was prepared to comprehend what she was about to hear.

"I've been doing some digging, just like you asked me to. I think this all goes back to the Reginald Peterson case."

"The contractor who was taken hostage a few months ago?" Bailey asked. It had been all over the news. Anyone who turned on the TV would have heard about the man.

He'd been hired by the government to do some work in the Middle East. But terrorists had grabbed him and demanded a hefty ransom. The man still hadn't been returned last she'd heard, but at least he was alive. She'd seen a video taken of him where he possessed a swollen eye, a bloody lip and an invisible yet unbearable weight on his shoulders.

"Yes, that Reginald Peterson," Micah responded. "But he wasn't just a government contractor. He was CIA."

"The CIA never owned up to it that he was one of their own, though," Ed filled in.

"Why would they do that?" Bailey asked.

Ed and Micah exchanged another glance.

"There was a rumor that Reginald had uncovered some evidence that incriminated the CIA," Ed answered. "He discovered something and sent it to his handler. He was abducted a few days later and that's when the CIA claimed they didn't know him.

"You have to understand that it's not surprising. I mean, if the interests of a nation are at stake, the CIA is going to do whatever they have to do to cover themselves. We believe that the information Reginald uncovered was one of the reasons he was abducted. The terrorists wanted that intelligence."

"Did he risk his life for the US, only to have the US turn their back on him?" Bailey asked.

"We don't know yet, nor do we know exactly what that information is he obtained," Ed said. "We believe that information was brushed under the rug by the CIA, but that Reginald's handler passed the information on to Elmer Martin. He then gave it to my father. Now they're all dead."

"So, if we get the information…?" Bailey could fill in the blanks a little too easily. She didn't like the answers she formulated. They all went back to the same conclusion: death.

"Whatever the communication is, it's raised the stakes for some high-level people within the CIA," Micah finished.

"You don't know what this intelligence is?" Bailey asked.

"We suspect it has to do with some kind of scandal or cover-up, possibly within the CIA," Micah said. "We also suspect that Carl Sanderson might be involved."

"Isn't he a terrorist?" Bailey tried to recall what she'd heard about him. Apparently, he had a whole army of followers. He was British, but had lived in Africa and the Middle East. The only other thing Bailey could remember was that he hated America. Apparently, he blamed the country for the death of his brother, who'd been a British double agent.

"Not only would it look bad for certain members of the CIA, but if the wrong people got their hands on that information, they could use it to put agents into compromising positions," Ed explained. "They could use it as leverage to get other information."

"That would be…not good." Bailey knew how lame her words sounded.

"You have to understand that given the scope of what the CIA does, something like this could mean the safety of our country," Micah added. "It's more than about people's reputations or smearing the image of the CIA. This is about keeping our country out of harm's way."

"And now we're involved somehow," Bailey said, her head still spinning.

"Someone's after this information. Could even be the CIA," Ed said.

"If the CIA sent people after us, that means someone had to own up to what happened, right?" Bailey tried to put it all together.

"Not necessarily," Ed said. "They could have concocted a story painting us as the bad guys. There are a lot of ways to spin the mission of an operation. They could have claimed that we stole information. That we're the threats to national security."

"Why would you kill your own father, though?" Bailey asked. "That's essentially what they'd have to claim in order to put the blame on us."

"There are holes we haven't filled in yet," Micah said. "I don't have all the answers."

"Do you know if there have been any threats made? Has anyone owned up to having the information? Any terrorist groups?" Ed asked.

"All indications are that this is an inside job."

Bailey ran a hand through her hair. "This is great. We have CIA assassins chasing us. I guess they were the ones at the house earlier? The ones who didn't kill us when they had the chance?"

"The bottom line is that someone wants this information. They want to stop the information flow. If we're dead, they still won't know where the information is, but they'll just try other means to find it."

Bailey remembered her sister, the threat on her family's lives. Yes, whoever was behind this was ruthless and heartless. They would do whatever it took to get their hands on the information.

They left an hour later. Micah had offered to let them stay at his place, but Ed knew it would put his friend at too much risk. They needed to put distance between themselves and everyone else—at least, for the moment. Micah was smart; he knew how to defend himself. He'd been an army ranger at one time—one of the best. Then he'd joined the CIA.

Ed found a hotel—one with outside doors. He booked two rooms side by side and paid with cash. He wasn't on the run; he wouldn't stay in hiding forever. But he had to take every precaution possible.

"Nice place," Bailey muttered, looking up at the outdated sign as Ed unlocked the door.

"They didn't ask for credit-card information, so it should work for the time being."

He ushered Bailey inside her room and locked the doors behind them. "Stay here," he ordered.

He checked every available spot in the room, just to make sure everything was safe. Finally, he let himself relax a moment. The hotel wasn't the fanciest, but it was the best option. "Everything looks clear. I'm just taking every precaution possible to make sure you're safe."

Bailey still stood against the wall, nearly pressed against it. "I'm scared, Ed."

He stepped closer to her and hooked a lock of hair behind her ear. "I know. You should be. Fear is healthy. It keeps you sharp and alert. That said, it's not fun, and I'm sorry about that."

"Why do you seem so calm?" Her wide eyes implored him, made him want to pour out everything.

"Experience."

"As a lawyer." She smiled slightly.

"Yeah, as a lawyer." Ed had no doubt that Bailey had put the facts together and knew there was quite a bit more to his job than that, especially given all the talk about the CIA.

She rubbed her arms and looked around. He had to admit that the room was cold; the heat needed to be kicked up another notch. He strode across the room to adjust the settings.

"Do you think they'll find us here?" she asked.

He cranked the heat up. "We're going to be ready for them if they do."

Against his better instinct, he pulled her toward him. Instantly, the smell of daisies and rain showers filled his senses. He liked the way she seemed to fold into him, a sweet-smelling bundle of warmth.

At once, he had visions of the future, hopes of forever.

Forever was a prospect he hadn't considered in a long time—long enough that the thought shook him to the core.

He stepped back, a little too quickly. The action rocked Bailey, and she struggled to find her balance. As he grabbed her, trying to help her right herself, another surge of electricity shot through him.

This wasn't good. It wasn't good at all.

He needed to do some reconnaissance on behalf of his heart.

He squeezed her arms before backing up and pointing to the door behind him. "I should be going. If you need anything, let me know."

Bailey nodded and rubbed her neck. "I'll do that."

"And lock these doors behind me."

He took a deep breath and stepped outside. There had been a lot of things he hadn't expected, starting with his father's death. But he definitely hadn't been prepared for his heart to feel this invested.

Bailey hardly slept all night. It'd been a common theme for her the past few nights. There was the fact that a crazy gunman was after them. And as if that wasn't enough, there was also the possibility of a CIA assassin, double agents, international hostages and plots to take over the world.

Add to that the fact that Ed's touch had ignited something in her that she hadn't felt in a long time. She was so used to being on her own, of taking care of herself, of as if someone else had her back. She hadn't realized how much her heart yearned for that protection.

She lay in bed for most of the night with her covers pulled up to her neck, listening for signs of anything suspicious. She heard nothing, except maybe a pizza delivery guy a few doors down.

When she'd finally pulled herself out of bed in the

morning, she'd frowned when she looked in the mirror and saw the dark circles under her eyes. This whole situation was beginning to wear on her. She took a shower and used the complimentary toothbrush and toothpaste to freshen up.

The fact that nothing had happened both put her at ease and more on edge. She'd fully expected some kind of attack. What did this mean?

She knocked on the door between her room and Ed's, crossing her arms as she waited for him to answer. Her heart skipped a beat when he pulled the door open. Based on the way his pupils widened, he was feeling the same thing she was.

They were both in trouble, in more ways than one.

"You okay?" he asked. His gaze soaked her in.

She nodded, noting how his hair glistened as if he'd just gotten out of the shower. "Yeah, I'm fine."

He grabbed his keys and motioned toward the outside door. "We should probably hit the road, then."

He put a hand on her back and led her through the room and to the door. He stepped outside first, glanced around and then led her to the car. They climbed inside. Bailey held her breath as he cranked the engine.

When the car purred to life, she nearly laughed out loud. What had she expected? An explosion? Maybe she'd watched too many movies.

With that worry over, the same raw feeling returned to her throat. She knew what had caused the achiness—her closeness to Ed. She wished her reaction to the man wasn't this strong. She wished it made more sense. She wished circumstances were different; that she was different.

She had to stay focused. She had to find that information.

And then what?

Turn it over to potential terrorists? Or people who were putting the security of the United States on the line?

Great. She could save her own family, but fail the entire country if she did.

She had some decisions to make. Some really, really hard decisions.

She rubbed her temples, wishing she could rewind time.

"What are you thinking about?"

Ed's voice pulled her from her burdensome thoughts. If only she could share what she was thinking about. "Just about how crazy all of this is."

"You've been a real trouper, you know. The smartest choice for you right now would be to pack your things and get out of here."

"You don't think they'd follow me? That they might suspect I somehow know something?"

He grimaced. "They might."

"I'm in this too deep, Ed. Whether I want to be in it or not, I'm involved. It sounds like the people behind this are desperate. It's like something from a movie."

"I know how they think, Bailey. I'll look out for you."

They reached the docks, finally. Ed's boat floated right where they'd left it, and there wasn't a sign of anyone else there at the moment.

The day was a little warmer than the past several had been. But the breeze still felt cool, and as they raced across the water, it would feel even colder.

They climbed onto the boat and, a few minutes later, were cruising toward Smuggler's Cove. Bailey stood beside Ed by the boat's console. The guard blocked the wind and the sun warmed her cheeks. Maybe this would be a decent ride. Maybe, just for a minute, she could forget her troubles.

Just then, an explosion rocked the entire boat.

Before Bailey realized what was happening, water surrounded her.

SEVENTEEN

Ed's head jetted from the water and he gulped in a deep breath. Debris from the boat floated around him and the smell of gas remained heavy on the water.

Where was Bailey?

He twisted around, searching for a sign of her. "Bailey!"

Nothing.

He swam closer to the wreckage, desperately looking for proof of life. Finally, he saw something pink. Her shirt?

He propelled himself across the water. The mop of long hair confirmed it was Bailey.

Moving quickly, he flipped her over. Her motionless, pale face caused panic to jostle through him. "Bailey, Bailey! You've got to stay with me."

She remained unmoving.

He patted her cheek, desperation surging through him. "Bailey!"

She still wasn't responding. Ed grabbed the largest piece of debris he could find—part of the bottom of the boat—and dragged Bailey on top of it. He didn't have much time. He had to move quickly.

Dear God, please help her!

He turned her on her side and pounded her back, praying the water would leave her lungs, that breath would fill her.

Nothing.

He kept trying.

Finally, she sputtered. Coughed. Tried to sit up.

He grabbed her arm to prevent her from rolling back into the water. She was okay. Praise God, she was okay!

The cut on her forehead would heal, but there were no other visible wounds. He prayed that was the extent of her injuries.

As she slid from the wreckage, his arm went around her waist, trying to hold her up. "You okay?"

"I…" She glanced around. "I thought I was dead."

He had, too. For a moment, at least. "You're going to be fine."

Now that she was awake and breathing, a new challenge rushed to his mind. How were they going to get out of the water? Out of the bay? The frigid water would give them hypothermia if they stayed here too long.

Bailey's teeth chattered. The cold was already getting to her, and their options weren't many. Swim for shore or stay here and wait for help. The problem was that no one would be looking for them. His only hope was in the realization that the route they'd traveled was a popular boat path for people going to and from Smuggler's Cove.

"Ed?" Bailey whispered, her skin too pallid for his comfort.

"Yes?"

"I…I want to say thank-you." Her teeth chattered.

"Oh, no. You're not giving me a goodbye speech. We're going to make it out of here." He continued to tread water, his muscles straining from the constant motion.

"I can't feel my hands anymore, Ed."

His worry grew.

Lord, please help.

He grabbed another piece of the boat and instructed Bailey to hang on to it. Keeping one arm around her so she wouldn't slide off, he began swimming toward the island. Making it there was a long shot. They were probably ten miles away, at least. But he had to try. He had to do something.

There had to have been a detonator on that boat. Someone must have planted it last night. They'd waited until Ed and Bailey came back to the boat and, when they were sure the watercraft was in the middle of the bay, they'd set it off.

At first, it seemed as if the people behind these acts wanted to keep them alive. But maybe now they were getting desperate. Whoever these guys were, they were realizing that Ed and Bailey were putting the pieces together.

He had to keep moving. If Bailey died, he would be to blame. He'd never forgive himself.

He glanced over at her. Her lips were turning blue. Her face was still pale.

The water was too cold. She was losing blood through the cut on her forehead. The exertion was too much.

He paused as a noise caught his ear.

He swerved his head around, looking for the source of the hum.

"It's a boat!" he said.

"Good guys or bad guys?" Bailey asked lethargically.

Ed kept his gaze on the watercraft. Finally, a symbol on the side registered with him. "Good guys. It's the coast guard."

Instead of going to Smuggler's Cove, the coast guard had taken them to the mainland, to a hospital outside of Richmond. Bailey kept insisting she was fine, but no one seemed to believe her.

The doctor decided to keep her and Ed overnight for observation. She had a cut on her forehead, which had caused her to lose blood. That, mixed with the hypothermia, were their reasons for concern.

Against her will, she'd drifted to sleep. But during her

waking hours, all she could think about was the men who were after them. What if they found her here at the hospital? What if they tried to finish what they started?

She couldn't fight the effects of the pain medicine and remain lucid enough to put up a fight.

Three hours after they were admitted, someone rapped at the door. She looked over and saw Ed standing there. His hair looked messy, he needed to shave, and his gaze looked tired. But was she ever glad to see him. Especially the lazy smile that stretched across his face when he spotted her.

"Hey, there," she called, her voice strained and weak.

He stepped up to her bed. "I was afraid you'd be sleeping."

"I keep drifting off, but then I wake up with nightmares."

His smile slipped. "How are you feeling?"

"My head throbs and my whole body feels like it's been wrung out by a tornado. But besides that, I'm just happy to be alive."

"I know the feeling."

Her throat got that all-too-familiar aching feeling. "Thank you, by the way," she whispered. "For saving my life."

"It was nothing."

"It was everything to me."

He looked down, something tortured in his gaze for a minute. "I just wish you weren't wrapped up in all of this. What happened out there on the water made this all too real, in more ways than one."

"Whether we like it or not, at this point, we're in this together. I'm just glad that was the case when that bomb went off in the boat. If you hadn't been there, I wouldn't be here right now."

Using his palm, he wiped her hair back from her forehead. "You gave me a good scare."

His touch sent ripples ricocheting through her. Her blood surged, warming her skin, making her long for more of his touch.

She cleared her throat, trying to get control of her reactions. She needed safe territory, somewhere where the look in Ed's eyes wouldn't make her heart betray her. Since that wasn't an option, she changed the subject. "So, do the police have any clue what happened? Are they investigating?"

"I told them what happened. I just didn't share any of the background. It doesn't matter, though. Not really. They're not going to catch these guys. They're too good."

"If they're not going to catch them, then how are we supposed to get out of this alive?"

He squeezed her hand. "Never give up. We've got to keep pressing ahead. God often steps in at our lowest moments and shows us another way. For example, if that coast guard boat hadn't come by when it did, neither of us may have made it."

Her first real smile came easily and quickly. "You're right."

"Mr. Carter," a nurse said, sticking her head into the room. "I thought I told you that you needed to stay in your room with your IV."

"I feel fine." He straightened, rubbing his arm where it seemed his IV had been.

"You really need to rest." The gray-haired nurse put her hands on her ample hips.

He pointed to the chair beside Bailey. "I'll rest in here."

"But—"

He raised a hand as if to say *Hold on.* "I promise. I'll be fine."

The nurse looked at Bailey, agitation clearly written across her face. "Do you want me to get rid of him for you?"

She smiled, despite her cracked lips and depleted energy. "No, he can stay. But thank you."

The nurse raised an eyebrow and cast one more glance at Ed before finally nodding and stepping out of the room.

Ed turned back to Bailey and patted her hand. "I'm here. You can rest now. I'll keep an eye out."

Surprisingly, Bailey found waves of assurance in those words.

The next morning, John met them at the hospital with some clean clothes and two prepaid cell phones that Ed had requested he pick up. Since they'd missed church, Ed and Bailey had read some Scripture together and lifted up a prayer. It felt good to have someone willing to worship with him, Ed mused.

After they'd changed and were discharged, John drove them from the hospital to his boat. Ed was thankful that the man had been willing and available. He felt better knowing that he was former coast guard.

Before climbing into the boat, Ed checked out every inch of it. He didn't see anything suspicious. As they took off across the water, Bailey clutched Ed's arm. Based on her tight grip, she was reliving yesterday. He put his arm around her waist and squeezed, wishing he could somehow ease her thoughts.

He appreciated the fact that John didn't ask too many questions. The former Coastie seemed to sense that the situation was tense, and he respected the unspoken boundaries—at least for the time being.

The day was warm, which helped melt some of his tension. These few stolen moments when Ed was able to forget the danger they were in seemed to refresh him.

He breathed easier when they glided up to the pier in Smuggler's Cove and anchored there. Ed helped Bailey out, hating the bruises on her face and the thick bandage across her forehead. But it could have been worse. Much worse.

Samantha came running down the pier and gave Bailey a hug. "Are you okay? I was so worried."

Bailey nodded, holding on to her friend's arm as they started toward the beach. "I'm fine."

"Is there anything I can do?"

He saw Bailey about to shake her head, and he stepped forward. "There is something. Could Bailey stay here, in one of the cabins?"

"Ed—" Bailey protested.

"I'm not sure how safe the house is," Ed whispered.

"But—" she began.

He leaned closer and lowered his voice. "I'd feel better if you were away from the place for a while."

Bailey narrowed her eyes, obviously feeling a little better if some of her fire was returning. "Can I speak with you a moment?"

With a hand at her elbow, he walked with her across the sand. He could only imagine what this conversation would hold.

They stopped, and she crossed her arms. "You really think I'm going to be any safer here?"

"Yes, I do." He had no doubt.

"What makes you think these guys aren't going to find me here? And you won't be around to bail me out next time."

"I just don't want to see you hurt again." He had to make her understand that.

"Staying here won't insure that."

He stared at her, trying to make the best decision, trying to give her the respect she deserved. "You're a big girl. It's your choice."

Her face seemed to relax before she jutted her chin out

with stubborn determination. "Then I choose to stay at the house."

He hesitated but then nodded. "Okay. If that's what you want."

They walked back toward John and Samantha, what almost felt like a physical weight pressing down on Ed.

Bailey spoke first. "I can't put you guys in the line of fire."

"You know we're there for you if you need us," John said. "We've been in tough spots before. We know what it's like."

"You can say that again," Samantha added.

"I appreciate it, but I couldn't forgive myself if something happened to any of you."

Ed's hand went to her back. He was doing that a lot lately. Something about being able to touch her made him feel connected, as if he was close enough to protect her. "She's right. It's better if we keep our distance."

"Do you want to tell us what's going on?" John asked, squinting against the midmorning sun.

"It's better if you don't know. Believe me, I'd tell you if I could." Ed knew they couldn't get anyone else involved. The less people who knew, the better it would be for everyone.

"You know where to find us," Samantha insisted.

His back muscles tightened as he nodded his thanks and waved goodbye. He was ready to head home. Though the way things were, he wasn't sure what else—or who else—to expect when he arrived.

EIGHTEEN

The night was quiet, and Bailey slept surprisingly well, but that was mostly because Ed was stationed outside her door. He wouldn't be able to keep up that schedule for long, though. Despite his toughness, his energy and clearheadedness would wane soon.

Today, the two could work together to find that information, those secret files that had been supposedly passed on to Mr. Carter. The only problem was that Bailey needed to find it first—before Ed. She had to hand it over to the man. She had no other choice.

Every time she closed her eyes, she pictured her sister and her niece and nephew. She couldn't put them at risk.

Yet she couldn't put the safety of a country at risk, either.

The thought was enough to make her stomach slosh with nausea. This whole experience was like waking up in a nightmare. She had no idea how to navigate her way out. Her only comfort was in knowing that God—and Ed—was by her side.

Though Ed had opened up to her—and she felt she understood him better—part of her still remained cautious around him. Though he hadn't outright said it, she knew he worked for the CIA. He lied for a living. She only hoped he wasn't fooling her now.

She lay in bed for a moment, her body still sore from

the crash. She and Ed could have easily died, she realized. God had obviously been watching out for them. She only prayed that He would continue to watch out for them.

The whole situation felt like a ticking time bomb. If Ed weren't beside her, doing this with her, then she wasn't sure she'd be able to handle it, either mentally or physically. He'd been her rock over the past couple of days, a realization that was crazy in itself.

Maybe, just maybe, she'd been wrong about him.

She opened the door from her room and blinked when she saw the hall was empty. Cautiously, she stepped out.

"Ed?" she called.

Silence answered.

She crept down the hallway, remaining on alert.

Moving slowly, she went downstairs. Nothing appeared out of place. There were no signs of struggle.

So where was Ed?

She tiptoed into the kitchen. A pot of coffee waited there. She couldn't wait to pump some of that caffeine into her system.

But first she had to figure out where Ed had gone.

Just then, the back door opened. Ed stood there, his hair moist with dew and the earthy scent of grass and seawater saturating him. He wiped his feet on the rug.

"Bailey. You're awake."

She let out a small laugh, chiding herself for her overreaction. "I'm here. I was worried when I didn't see you."

"I was just sweeping the place again, making sure there was nothing suspicious I needed to be aware of. I did the inside earlier, and I decided to take a look outside this morning."

She crossed her arms, telling herself it was to ward away chills. "Anything?"

He shook his head. "Surprisingly, no. Everything looks clean."

"Strange when you consider they had a whole twenty-four hours to set their little traps."

He shrugged. "Maybe they were too busy trying to follow us."

His words didn't sound convincing, though. Certainly the network they were using was larger than one or two people. If these people had wanted someone here, they could have had someone here.

Ed stepped inside and pointed to the fridge. "Mr. Wilkins dropped some groceries by here."

"Mr. Wilkins did?" Bailey opened the fridge. She'd never known the man to buy food and stock the place.

"I asked him to. I think he appreciates the additional income."

Bailey nodded. That made sense.

"After breakfast, I say we go through the house again and see if there's anything my father left that might give us a hint as to what was going on. Maybe look for those letters. My father's friend obviously either told him or gave him some kind of information. There's a good chance it's still here. If we're able to find it, maybe we can figure out a resolution to all of this."

Bailey nodded. "That sounds good to me."

Ed grabbed an apron that was hanging on the wall, a red one with polka dots. "Now, how about if I fix some breakfast?"

Bailey smiled, some of her tension easing for a moment. "That sounds perfect."

Four hours later, Ed paused and stared at Bailey a moment, resisting the urge to wipe away the dust smudged on her cheek. She sat back on the floor of the library and let out a long sigh, her hair escaping from the loose ponytail that held it back.

"Nothing. We've searched everything, everywhere I can possibly think of."

Ed stood and stretched. "Let's take a break. Maybe some fresh air will help us think more clearly."

He reached for her hand and pulled her to her feet. When she popped up, they were standing closer than he'd anticipated—close enough that electricity crackled between them.

Against his better instincts, he reached forward and, using his knuckles, wiped away that smudge. "Dust," he explained.

Based on the look in her eyes, she felt just as electrified as he did.

"Thank you," she muttered.

At once, his arm went around her waist. He leaned forward, waiting for Bailey to object, giving her a moment to back away. When she didn't, his lips met hers.

Something about the two of them fit so well together. He could get used to her soft skin, her sweet smell and her compassionate eyes.

When they pulled away, Bailey tucked herself into his arms. "We shouldn't have done that, should we?"

"Says who?" He rubbed her back.

"Common sense perhaps."

"Circumstances like this…they can accelerate feelings. I know it sounds crazy. We've only known each other a few days, but—"

"But I've never felt like this before, which is in some ways scarier than the fact that there are people out there who want to kill us."

He stepped back, wanting to look Bailey in the eye. "I won't hurt you, Bailey."

Her eyes flashed with something. Doubt? Distrust? Skepticism? He couldn't be sure. But, more than anything, he wanted to put her worries at ease.

"I hope that's true," she finally whispered.

He grabbed her hand. "Come on. Let's go outside."

Maybe they both needed to clear their heads.

They didn't say anything as they both seemed to instinctively head toward the beach.

Halfway across the lawn, Bailey stopped. "What's that on the sand over there?"

Ed squinted toward the distance. There was a lump of black and white on the shore. It could simply be something that washed up from the ocean—a creature, trash, even seaweed.

"I don't know," he said. "Let's go check it out."

They picked up their pace and hurried toward the sandy banks. The closer they got, the more clearly Ed realized that the lump was not trash or seaweed.

The lump was a body.

A dead body.

NINETEEN

Bailey stared down at the lifeless man, emotions colliding inside her. She felt an uneven mix of anxiety, dread and forewarning that she just couldn't shake. Now there was a dead body that had washed up outside of the Carter house.

Things weren't going to get better. Not until the information was found. Not until the bad guys were behind bars.

There was no going back and no hoping that things would work themselves out or that these people would go away. And that thought made her feel off balance.

They called the sheriff, and he arrived at the scene fifteen minutes later.

"So, you have no idea who this man is?" Sheriff Davis asked.

Ed shook his head. "I've never seen him before."

"And you, Bailey?" The sheriff turned toward her. His eyes were shielded by his sunglasses, but she'd always known the sheriff to be a fair man. He was simply investigating this death now. She knew there would be no accusation in his gaze.

That was what she tried to tell herself, at least.

Things like dead bodies washing ashore just didn't happen here on Smuggler's Cove. This would be the story of the decade, maybe even the century.

She still clutched her throat, unable to get the image of the man out of her mind. "No, I have no idea. He looks a little like that man who was working down at the docks, doesn't he?"

Ed looked closer. "Now that you mention it, he kind of does."

Bailey shook her head, resisting the urge to cry. "It's hard to tell. He's awfully swollen."

"You have a name for this dockworker?"

"I think it was Arnold. I thought he was watching me one day while we were down there and when we tried to talk to him about it, he ran," Bailey explained.

The sheriff bent down toward the rumpled heap of a man, who wore a black coat with jeans and boots. There was clearly a bullet hole going through his temple. Was this the man from the docks? She couldn't be sure. Even if it was him, why was he dead? What had happened? Did this relate in some way to everything else that was going on?

Using a pen, the sheriff opened the man's jacket. From where Bailey stood, she saw a wallet peeking out from an inside pocket. The sheriff pulled on some gloves and carefully pulled it out. As he opened the fold, something fluttered to the ground. A paper. Maybe a photo.

Bailey stepped closer, anxious to see what it was.

She gasped when the object came into focus.

It was a picture.

Of Ed.

The sheriff looked up at the two of them. "You sure you don't want to revise your earlier statement?"

Thoughts collided inside Bailey's head. Ed had been outside this morning. He had a gun. He'd probably used that gun in precarious situations before.

Could Ed have killed that man?

She shook her head, trying to clear her thoughts. Just an hour earlier, she'd been longing for forever with the man. Or, at least, the possibility of it. She'd been feeling things she hadn't felt in years and was beginning to trust.

Now, with one picture, all of that started to vanish.

You're being ridiculous, Bailey, she scolded herself. *There's probably another explanation for this. Maybe someone is trying to frame Ed.*

"Sheriff, we didn't get back here until late yesterday afternoon," Ed said. "Bailey and I both were checked into a hospital because of a boating accident, so they can verify my presence there. Bailey and I were here for the rest of the evening, trying to get my father's estate in order."

"And this morning?" Sheriff Davis pulled his sunglasses down, his gaze clearly showing that he meant business.

"The man has been dead for longer than today." He pointed to the body. "He's waterlogged, rigor mortis has set in. This crime didn't happen this morning."

"And what did you say you did for a living again?"

Ed didn't flinch. "I'm a lawyer."

"And you know all about dead bodies how?"

Ed shrugged. "Watching crime dramas on TV? I don't know. Everyone knows that information."

He was doing a good job playing as if he didn't know. He was good at skirting the truth. Certainly he had to be in his line of work.

"How about you, Bailey?" The sheriff turned toward her. "Did you know that?"

Panic raced through her. Guilt flashed through her that, only minutes before, she'd been questioning Ed's guilt. "He…he has good points, Sheriff. My guess, based on my experience as a nurse, is that this man has been dead for several hours, and out to sea for longer than that."

"And the fact that he washed up here?" the sheriff continued.

Bailey shrugged. "It could have happened anywhere on the island, really. The tide just happened to be working against us and washed him up here."

Sheriff Davis held up the picture. "How did your picture end up in his wallet, then?"

Ed shook his head. "I wish I could tell you that. I have no idea. Like I said, if this is the man from the docks, then I've never spoken with him."

A few hours later, Bailey finally found some time by herself and she called her sister. She climbed up to the widow's walk, her favorite place, to clear her head. She nestled down on the lone bench and held her breath, waiting for Lauren to answer and making a mental note to water the spider plant sometime that day.

When her sister's voice finally sounded across the line, Bailey let out a long, relieved sigh. "How are you, Lauren?"

"Busy as ever, but we're doing okay. How about you? You coming back for a visit anytime soon?"

"I'm trying to wrap things up here. As soon as I'm done, I'll come for a visit." She glanced out the widow's walk and saw the police were still there collecting evidence. The horrors of the past week still made her head spin. How had everything spun out of control?

"Your patient must have left a lot of loose ends. I didn't think this was in your job description."

"It's not. Officially, at least. But someone's got to do it, and I'm already here. Besides, I don't mind." Originally she wanted to help for Mr. Carter's sake. But now she knew Ed, and she wanted to help him.

"Did the man's son ever show up?" Lauren asked.

Ed's picture flashed in her mind. "He did. I've been helping him."

"Would serve him right it he had to do it all by himself. That's what he deserves for missing his own father's funeral."

Bailey's cheeks flushed. That was what she'd thought

at one time, also. "He actually had a decent excuse for not being here, and he felt terrible about it."

Her sister paused. "Wow, what's that in your voice? I want to say compassion, but that's not quite it. Is Mr. Carter's son handsome, by chance?"

"Lauren!" Bailey's cheeks heated even more. "Yes, he is. But that's not why I'm defending him. You know me better than that."

"You're right, sis. You're not superficial. You always see the best in people, for that matter. Speaking of which, I got the strangest knock at my door the other day."

Familiar apprehension stretched across her shoulders. "Is that right? Who was it?"

"It was some guy who worked for the city and he was surveying all the yards in the neighborhood for something. Anyway, he said he used to know you."

Familiar tension filled her. "How did he know who you were? We have different last names now that you're married. Plus, I've never lived in Florida."

"I know. Weird, right? He was a real friendly guy. We just started talking. He said we look alike. Isn't that crazy?"

Her sister was a petite brunette. "That's crazy. But, all that said, I have no idea who you're talking about. Is the world that small that someone I dated in North Carolina is now down in Florida?"

"He said his name was Vince."

"I don't ever remember dating a Vince. And I would remember."

"Let's see if this rings any bells. He was super tall. Probably six-three. He looked like he works out, he had light brown hair, kind of spiky, and a killer smile."

If her sister only realized the implications of that last cliché. The only person who fit that description was Ed's friend Micah. He had said he'd just gotten in from out of town. Could he be the person at the CIA who was in on this?

"Bailey? You there?"

Bailey snapped back to the present. "Nope. He still doesn't ring any bells. I don't think I've ever dated anyone who fits that description."

"Maybe it'll come to you while you sleep tonight. A college boyfriend? Blind date? I don't know. He couldn't have been making it up. He knew too much about you."

Bailey's throat tightened even more. "Did he? Like what?"

"For one thing, he knew you were in Smuggler's Cove now, so he must be someone you've spoken with in the past year."

Her heart pounded in her ears. She forced her voice to sound light. "Maybe he was that guy I met at a picnic right before I left. I, uh, I didn't know him well, but I didn't get good vibes from him. If he comes back, I'd stay away from him, Lauren."

She prayed her sister would understand.

Bailey knew the truth—the man was one of the bad guys, and he clearly wanted Bailey to know exactly what his reach was.

Those threats weren't empty; this man fully planned on carrying out his mission unless Bailey did exactly what he said.

TWENTY

Ed hung up with his friend Archie just as Bailey came back into the living room. The whole situation was becoming precarious, and he didn't know whom he could trust anymore. Archie had never let him down before, though.

Finding the information seemed a futile task. Now there was that dead body that had washed up on the shore. Ed had a feeling that the man was Arnold, the dockworker. What he didn't know was why he might have been killed or by whom. Had the man betrayed them? Made a fatal mistake that had sealed his destiny?

Even more worrisome was the fact that Ed's picture was in the man's wallet. Would he be framed for this? The state police had been called in, and there would be an investigation into the matter. This was more than one sheriff on the island could handle. Who knew what other kind of evidence had been planted? He certainly didn't.

Just then, someone knocked at the door. Ed motioned for Bailey to stay back; he would answer, just in case. He was surprised when he saw Todd standing on the stoop there.

"I have those windows. I'm sure you're anxious to replace that wood in your kitchen, especially since they're calling for thunderstorms over the next several nights."

He opened the door more. "Please. Come in."

Todd glanced at Bailey and nodded. "Bailey. How are you?"

She smiled, though the action looked strained. "Hanging in."

"I heard about the body that washed up on the shore. It's been the talk of the island."

Ed had to play it cool so he didn't raise suspicions. "Crazy, isn't it?"

"Yeah, stuff like that doesn't happen around here. It's already got everyone on edge. Between that and all the visitors we've seen around here lately."

"Visitors?" Ed asked.

Todd nodded. "Yeah, this usually isn't tourist season, but there have been some people staying at the bed-and-breakfast in town. They don't really seem like the remote-fishing-island type of people, more like the New York City type."

"Anyone know why they're here?" Ed kept his voice even.

Todd shrugged. "*Were* here. They left two days ago. They were supposedly on a marriage retreat."

"So, it was a man and a woman?" Bailey asked, glancing at Ed.

"Yeah, a younger couple. Anyway, almost everyone in town was speculating about them. You know how small towns are." Todd sat down his toolbox on the kitchen table.

Ed crossed his arms and leaned against the counter. "I suppose I'm the source of some of the speculation."

Todd laughed, but the noise sounded too forced. "I can't deny it. Rumor has it that you were running around in Europe, cavorting with kings and diplomats."

"People have wild imaginations, don't they? And here I am, just a boring lawyer."

Todd glanced back at Bailey. "And, of course, everyone thought Bailey would leave. Now they think the two of you have fallen in love or something."

Bailey let out a nervous laugh. "That's crazy."

"She's been a real godsend helping me out around here," Ed said.

"I'm getting paid," Bailey added.

Todd raised his eyebrows. Perhaps they were objecting too much.

He turned back to Ed as he unloaded his tools. "You selling this place?"

Ed shrugged. "I'm considering my options."

"Lots of people would like to have their hands on a piece of property like this."

"But not everyone could live without a car or access to a shopping mall."

"I can't argue with that." Todd turned back to the window. "So, anyway, this should take maybe an hour to put the windows in and caulk around the edges."

Ed nodded. "I'll give you a hand."

At this point, he didn't trust anyone easily. No way was he leaving this guy here by himself.

"Ed, can I have a moment?" Bailey asked.

He nodded and stepped down the hallway.

"Let me have a few minutes alone with him," she said.

"Why would I do that? I don't know if I can trust him. I don't want to leave him alone with you. He knew this house, Bailey. He's been in and out. He's a suspect in my mind."

"He might talk to me," she insisted. "Let me give it a shot."

"You really want to do this?" Ed stared at her, wanting to protect her, but knowing he had to trust her, as well.

She nodded. "I do."

Ed stepped back. "Okay. But I'm staying close, just in case."

Bailey and Ed walked back into the kitchen. Bailey took a deep breath, trying to tap into her best acting skills.

She reminded herself of the life-and-death implications of doing this and prayed that God would forgive her for this charade she was putting on.

"I'm going to go grab some things outside," Ed told Todd, continuing toward the back door. "I'll be right back."

"No hurry," Todd mumbled.

Bailey tried to look casual as she stood against the kitchen island.

Todd looked over and smiled. "You sticking around?"

"Why not?" She observed Todd, wondering if he was the person behind the footsteps Mary Lou had heard. He was too thin and lightweight, she concluded. Yet he wasn't telling the truth about something.

Todd pried the plywood from the window. "Yeah, why not?"

"I need to be honest, Todd. I have a question for you."

"Ask away."

She paused for just a moment, praying that she'd have the right words and approach. "Did you put in a walkway in the hayloft for Mr. Carter?"

His eyes flickered with surprise, but he kept working, not missing a beat. "Actually, I did."

"When did you do that?"

"Mr. Carter asked me to about a month ago."

"Why didn't I know about that? It seems odd that he would have kept that from me."

Todd shrugged. "I don't know. The whole project only took a day. I think you'd gone over to the mainland to pick up his prescriptions or something."

"Did he say why he needed a walkway up there?"

Todd shook his head. "It wasn't my business. He told me not to tell anyone about it, though."

Wasn't that interesting? There was something else that Todd knew that he wasn't sharing. Bailey wanted to know what. Before she could ask, Ed stepped back inside.

"Bailey, I just remembered something I need to get in town. I was wondering if you could go with me."

She stared at him, trying to read him. She wasn't through questioning Todd yet. Yet she could tell by Ed's gaze that he needed to talk to her.

"Sure," she finally muttered.

"We'll be back in thirty, forty minutes," Ed told Todd.

As soon as they were outside, Bailey turned to Ed. "What was that about?"

"We're not really leaving," Ed whispered as they stepped outside. "I heard the conversation from outside. He's hiding something."

"Yeah, I thought the same thing. I didn't have a chance to get enough information out of him before you interrupted."

"We're going to wait in those trees over there. If my hunch is correct, he's going to go out to the garage and do some investigating himself. Especially if he knows something."

"You think?"

He nodded.

They started down the pathway leading into town, but then skirted around the property of the house until they reached the side yard. They squatted there and waited.

Bailey thought about telling Ed about her conversation with her sister. She thought about mentioning that a man who looked like Micah had shown up at her sister's place. But if she shared that information, Ed might ask too many questions. He might put too many details together and realize that Bailey was more involved in this than she'd admitted.

The questions and choices battled in her mind. She wanted to be honest with him. But she also had to look out for her family. Her head pounded as she weighed her options.

Just when Bailey thought for sure that Ed was wrong, Todd stepped out the back door. He looked from side to side, as if searching for anyone watching. When he didn't see anyone, he stepped onto the grass and headed straight for...the garage!

"Just what is he up to?" Bailey muttered.

"He might be the culprit in all of this. You said he lied about not being in town, right?" Ed whispered.

She nodded. "Yeah, Samantha said she saw him. He told me he was out of town."

"Did you say he's former military?"

Bailey nodded. "He sure is."

"That only solidifies my suspicions."

As Todd disappeared into the garage, Ed stood. "Come on. We've got to stay quiet, though."

Bailey nodded. Ed took her hand and pulled her behind him. They stayed low as they approached the garage. Slowly, they slid in through the open barn door.

Footsteps sounded overhead. Someone was up there. *Todd* was up there.

Ed put a finger over his lips, motioning for her to be quiet. Bailey nodded as Ed pulled out his gun and crept toward the wooden ladder leading upstairs. With stealthlike quietness, he climbed upward. Bailey stayed behind, waiting for his signal to follow.

A moment later, he came back to the ladder. "I don't see him," Ed whispered.

"What do you mean? Where'd he go?" Bailey asked.

Ed shook his head. "I don't know. He's not up here."

Bailey climbed the ladder, desperate to see for herself. She knew she'd heard those footsteps. Todd was here somewhere. He didn't just disappear.

But when she reached the loft, what Ed said was confirmed. It was empty.

"What's going on?" Bailey whispered.

"I wish I knew."

Just then, the wall slid open and Todd stood there, an unreadable expression on his face.

"Please. I can explain," Todd started, raising his hands in the air. "Just don't shoot me."

"Then start talking," Ed groused.

"Your dad asked me to build this room. I didn't ask any questions. I just did as he asked." He stood in the doorway on the other side of the loft, frozen.

Ed observed how the wall was still made with old wood, so based on outer appearances, no one could tell there was anything different. He'd done a good job concealing the space.

"So, why did you sneak up here now?" Bailey asked.

"Mr. Carter told me I couldn't tell anyone this was here. Anyone. But now he's dead, and I wondered if there was something in here that I should know about."

"Why would you need to know about anything?" Ed asked.

"What if there were explosives in here? Or dead bodies? I don't know. Everyone on the island thought your dad was a spook. I had no idea what was in here. But now that he's not here, I thought it deserved a check."

Ed pointed with his gun toward the wall. "What's in there?"

Todd shrugged. "It's a darkroom."

"A darkroom?" Certainly Ed hadn't heard correctly.

Todd nodded. "Like a photographer might use to process pictures."

"And you're telling me my dad, who was in his sixties, came out here, climbed that ladder and went into a darkroom?" Something wasn't adding up. Ed just couldn't see his father doing that. Not unless it was for a really important reason.

"I never saw him do it. I can't imagine who else this room would be for."

Ed turned to Bailey. "You have any idea what this is about?"

"I'm just as perplexed as you are," she admitted. "It doesn't make any sense."

"You've got to believe me when I say I'm not guilty of anything here," Todd insisted. "I just wanted to check things out, make sure everything was okay in here."

"Todd, you told me you got back to the island on the day after the storm. Someone else told me they saw you here before the storm. Why did you lie?" Bailey asked.

"I didn't," he said. "I did come back two days before the storm. Then some people on the mainland hired me to help them board up their homes and prepare for high winds we were supposed to have, so I left again." He looked back and forth from Bailey and Ed. "What's going on here? Why do you have a gun anyway?"

"I can't tell you that."

"What…what are you going to do now?" Todd stared at the gun still.

"I haven't decided." Just as he said the words, something clicked in Ed's mind.

He knew why his father had a darkroom. He also knew why he had the microscope and the other equipment. There was only one reason his father would have risked coming up here. Only one reason why his father would want a hidden room.

"Todd, please go finish the window. I'll handle things here."

"You're not going to shoot me?"

Ed shook his head and put his gun away. "Of course not. What do you think, that I'm some kind of barbarian?"

Todd didn't say anything else. He simply scrambled past and hurried down the ladder.

Ed stared into the opening of the room. He knew exactly what he needed to look for. He just prayed to God he could find it.

TWENTY-ONE

Stepping into the room, Ed began looking around. Everything had fallen into place in his mind.

He searched through all the equipment, but didn't find anything. That meant his father had hidden the information, and that he'd hidden it well. Maybe too well. Like a needle in a haystack, which was fitting, since they were in a loft in a barn.

"Can you tell me what's going on?" Bailey asked. She leaned against the doorway with her arms crossed.

Ed paused, leaning against the table. "I can't tell you."

She shook her head, disillusionment in her gaze. "After everything we've been through together, you can't tell me?"

He wished he could. He really did. And most of the time, he thought he could trust Bailey. But every once in a while, he caught a glimpse of something in her eyes. Something that she was hiding.

And until he knew what that something was, he couldn't tell her about his realization. It was too risky. There was too much at stake.

"I'm sorry, Bailey. As soon as I can, I'll tell you."

She shook her head and straightened. "You're serious?"

He nodded, unable to ignore the accusation and hurt in her gaze. "It's complicated."

"I'd say." Her voice sounded just above a whisper.

He leaned closer and lowered his voice. "Bailey, why don't you tell me your secret? Then I'll share mine."

Her face went slack, and he knew he'd hit the nail on the head. She *did* have a secret. Was she working for the other side? Did she have some kind of personal stake in all of this?

"I can't," she whispered. Her eyes looked tortured as she looked up at him. Her voice trembled.

He closed the space between them, wishing he could read the look in her eyes a little better. She almost looked scared. But what reason would she have for being scared? "Why not? Why can't you tell me, Bailey?"

"It's complicated," she said, echoing his earlier words.

The two stared at each other a moment until finally Bailey stepped back, tears pouring down her cheeks. "I'm going to go make myself useful."

Ed's heart clutched with a mix of grief, betrayal and distrust. He never wanted to see Bailey cry again...but until they were both able to be honest with each other, he couldn't guarantee it wouldn't happen again.

Three hours later, Bailey's anxiety only continued to increase. The deadline that bully had given her was tomorrow. If she didn't find that information tonight, then her sister would die. Ed obviously knew something, but he wasn't sharing. Part of her couldn't blame him.

But despair was threatening to overtake her. She had to keep her sister safe; she simply had no idea how.

After Todd left, the state police stopped by to ask questions about the body found on shore. She and Ed remained cordial to each other, but it was obvious a wall had gone up between them.

As soon as it turned eight, Bailey stood and stretched. "I'm going to turn in for the evening. It's been a long day."

Ed nodded from the recliner, where he'd absently been staring at the fire. "Good night, then."

Just as she took a step away, he called her back. Bailey paused, holding her breath, secretly hoping that he would share something with her—something that would help.

"I just wanted you to know that my friend Micah may be stopping by tomorrow. He said he found out something, but he wants to share that information in person."

Alarm jolted through her. Was Micah who he claimed to be? Or was he working for the bad guys?

She nodded weakly, desperately needing to think things through. "Got it," she finally muttered.

Ed's gaze stayed on her, asking her silent questions that she didn't answer. He knew she was acting strange, and she wished more than anything that she could tell him the reasons why. But she couldn't. Not now. Maybe not ever.

She waited an hour after she heard Ed retreat to his room downstairs. The house finally went silent. She pictured Ed exhausted and falling into a deep sleep. That was probably wishful thinking, however. He was like a loyal guard dog—always on alert, always watching and anticipating.

Her best guess was still the library. Moving quietly, she opened her door and stepped out into the hallway. She gently pulled the door shut behind her and began tiptoeing down the hall.

Ed seemed to have animal-like instincts at times; she prayed he wouldn't hear her now.

She reached the library without a sign of anyone behind her. Maybe—just maybe—this would work. She could hope, at least. But if Ed found out she was keeping this secret, she feared he might kick her out of the house and never trust her again.

Not only would this "mission" be lost, but so would the start of what could have been a great relationship with Ed.

She'd felt secure, protected, cherished even. She hadn't felt that way in a long time—maybe ever. Though they'd only known each other a short time, she already couldn't imagine her life without him.

Moving quickly but quietly, she started from scratch, as if she'd never searched this room before. She looked in books, under knickknacks, in every crevice of the desk there.

She found nothing.

What was she even looking for? Papers? Files? A jump drive or a disk? She had no idea, which only made this more complicated. Maybe this information was on a picture. Would that explain the photo lab in the barn? She didn't know, and her head was spinning from exhaustion and stress.

Finally, she sat back on the floor, feeling defeated. She had no idea. She'd searched every part of this room she thought possible. Where did she go from here?

She closed her eyes and replayed Mr. Carter's last days, the days when he was still mobile. They'd gone for a couple of walks on the bay. They'd sat on the porch. They'd spent a lot of time in front of the fireplace.

Other than that, they'd done their usual. She'd read to him. They'd eaten meals together. He'd told her about the different places he'd been in the world.

Was there a clue in any of that? She didn't see how there could be.

She refused to let the tears that wanted to spill over escape onto her cheeks. She wasn't going to give up. Not yet. She'd fight this until the end.

She started back up to her room, needing to regroup. At the last minute, she headed up to the widow's walk. It'd been her sanctuary for weeks and maybe now it would help clear her head.

Quietly, she climbed the spiral staircase. At the top, she

found comfort in the fact that the area was relatively uncluttered. The only things in the space were a small padded bench and a plant that she'd promised to water. At least she had no fear of someone hiding up here.

That didn't stop apprehension from filling her as she took her first step.

No, no one would be hiding, but being up here did make her feel exposed. Since it was so dark outside, no one should be able to see her, she told herself.

She sat on the bench and pulled her knees to her chest, praying for some kind of answer or solution. She was plain out of ideas.

If that information were in the house, where would Mr. Carter have put it? They'd searched everywhere. Even the garage, the closets, drawers, under rugs and behind paintings.

The only place they hadn't searched was…up here.

This area was so empty, so sparsely decorated, that the thought had never occurred to them.

She stood. It was incredibly dark, but her eyes had adjusted some to the blackness. Her options were limited, but it was worth a shot.

She lifted the cushion of her bench and held her breath. There was nothing there.

She flipped the bench over and examined the bottom. Again, nothing.

Next, she looked under the rug and under the potted plant. She didn't find anything and familiar desperation began to set in.

The last thing she did was to pull the potted plant out of the decorative pot it had been placed in.

What she saw there made her suck in a deep breath.

It was a small, clear bag.

With something inside.

She carefully lifted it and broke the seal at the top. Inside, there were two envelopes. The first one had Ed's name on it. The second one had hers.

Her hands trembled as she opened the letter and pulled out a folded piece of paper. She held the note close, trying to make out the handwritten words. It was no use. It was just too dark, too hard to see.

She'd have to take the letters down to her room and read her letter there.

Anticipation zipped through her muscles and bones.

If this weren't the "information," maybe it would offer a clue as to what that information was or how to find it.

It made sense now. Mr. Carter knew she loved it up here. He had to figure she'd eventually discover this hiding spot. In fact, he'd said something about taking this plant with her if anything ever happened to him. She'd never put it together before.

She had to get downstairs and—

"I'll take those," someone said.

Bailey gasped and jumped back a step.

She looked up to see a man and woman standing at the door by the stairway. The man pointed a gun at her, while the woman had her hand outstretched, waiting for the letters. The woman was petite and thin with short black hair and a heart-shaped face. There was nothing heartlike about her eyes, though. They looked cold, calculating and like she could strike at any minute.

"Who are you?"

The man smirked. "Last-minute changes to a person's will can raise red flags."

Those were the same words that... Bailey swung her gaze toward the man and gasped. She fully expected to see A.J. Andrews.

But it wasn't. Or was it? He looked different. There was no cleft chin. His cheekbones weren't as high. His hair wasn't as full.

"A.J.?"

"The real A.J. Andrews is dead. He had an unfortunate accident. The man you spoke with at the office was my younger brother. Most people call me Sanderson."

"You're behind all of this?"

He smiled at her as if the answer to that question was obvious. "I figured in good time you'd lead me to the information. Good work, Bailey."

Bailey shook her head and pulled the letters closer to her chest. "They're just goodbye letters. Not information."

"If they're just goodbye letters, why don't you hand them over? It shouldn't be a big deal," the woman crooned, raising a thinly arched eyebrow.

"It's a big deal because they're mine, not yours." Bailey had to buy time. She had to think!

Sanderson cocked the gun. "Are you willing to give up your life for those letters?"

Bailey's shoulders tightened. "You're going to kill me anyway. I'm not naive."

The woman reached into her pocket and threw something at Bailey. She braced herself for a flare, an explosion…pain. Instead, she saw a flashlight roll at her feet.

"Read it out loud," the woman instructed.

"Who are you anyway?" Bailey asked as she reached down for the light.

"I wouldn't ask many questions right now," the woman said.

Bailey flicked the light on, trying to control the tremble in her hands.

The man and woman blocked the only entrance and exit from the room. They had a gun, and Bailey didn't. There were two of them and one of her.

This wasn't good, and she had no idea how to get out of the situation.

TWENTY-TWO

Ed paused at the staircase as voices drifted downward.

"This is the only thing I could find." Bailey. That was Bailey's voice, he realized.

"I don't see how this helps," someone else said. Another woman.

"I don't see how, either, but I've looked everywhere," Bailey said.

What? Bailey was secretly looking for the information on her own? Why would she do that...unless she was working for someone? Someone who wasn't on his side.

The pain of betrayal sliced through him again. When would he learn he couldn't trust people? Especially women.

The betrayal turned into a surge of anger.

He had to put an end to whatever secret meeting was going on up there.

"We were counting on you. You've disappointed me," a female voice sounded.

He froze in the stairway, just out of sight. Why did that voice sound familiar? Realization dawned on him. He knew that voice. He knew that voice well.

So well that the sound of that person made his blood turn cold.

Claire.

His ex-fiancée.

The one who was working for a terrorist organization.

She'd been in on all of this the whole time? But why? Unless she wanted the information Reginald had obtained. In the wrong hands, the wrong people could use it to bend diplomatic decisions. They could hold it as leverage over decision makers here in America.

"I'll take those papers," Claire said.

"Why?" Bailey said. "There's nothing there. You heard what's here. It's nothing."

"I'll be the judge of that."

"I just need more time," Bailey pleaded.

"We've given you plenty of time. We gave you one simple task and you failed."

"Please, there's got to be another way." Bailey's voice almost sounded laced with panic.

Had she sold out to the other side, and now she wanted to get back in their good graces? Maybe her working here wasn't a coincidence after all. Maybe she was a manipulator, just like nearly everyone else in his life had been.

He took a step back and contemplated his next move. He'd have to plan carefully, with no room for mistakes.

Bailey stared at the two people in front of her, still wondering how in the world she was going to get herself out of this situation.

"Take her down," Sanderson muttered, nodding toward Bailey.

"No!" Bailey yelled as the woman raised her gun.

Suddenly, someone flew into the room. Sanderson crashed onto the floor, but not before a bullet flew through the air. Glass shattered.

Ed. That was Ed.

Before Bailey could think twice, she ran toward the woman. She aimed low and her shoulder hit the woman's midsection. The two tumbled onto the ground.

It may have been her dumbest move ever, because in

one swift motion the woman had flipped over and had Bailey pinned against the floor. For a small woman, she was surprisingly strong and agile. She kept her elbow at Bailey's throat and sneered. "Not smart."

Bailey tried to suck in a breath but couldn't. The woman blocked her airway. Panic began to pool in her.

"Put down the gun, Ed, or I'll kill her," the woman growled. "You know I will."

Beyond the woman, Ed's face came into view. He held a gun, aimed at the woman. Slowly, he lowered the weapon to the floor. "Don't hurt her, Claire."

Claire…wasn't Claire the name of the woman who'd broken Ed's heart? Bailey felt fairly certain that was the case. So, Claire was a spy?

"Smart man," Claire murmured.

"Not as smart as I should have been." Ed turned toward Sanderson and scowled. "You're involved in this, too? I should have recognized you, Sanderson. I should have figured that when you went off the grid, you were planning something big."

"It's amazing what plastic surgery and a wig can do." Sanderson smirked. "I've wanted to kill you from the moment I laid eyes on you. I couldn't, though. Not until I got what I needed."

"You two were the couple at the bed-and-breakfast," Ed said.

Sanderson shrugged. "We figured it was only a matter of time until you figured it out."

"Why'd you kill the dockworker?" Ed continued, trying to buy time.

"He was actually CIA," Claire added. "He was keeping an eye on you, but he was onto us. He had to go."

"This information must be pretty important for you guys to go through all of this trouble." Ed stared back and forth from Sanderson to Claire to Bailey.

"You could say that," Sanderson grumbled.

"I think it's going to be a little too easy to have some fun with your little girlfriend here," Claire muttered, her voice taking on an all-too-delighted tone.

"You were in cahoots with them the whole time, Bailey?" Ed said, unable to forget her involvement in all of this. "Until they betrayed you. Never trust a spy."

Bailey sucked in a deep breath, realizing for the first time how this might look. "It's not like that."

"I heard your conversation earlier. You were trying to help them."

"It's a long story, Ed. It's not what you think. Please, you've got to believe me." Her voice quivered with desperation.

"It's okay, Bailey. I'm used to being stabbed in the back."

"Country always comes first, Ed," Claire crooned. "I'm sorry you had to learn that the hard way."

"You know, in the year since we broke up, I haven't regretted what happened. No, I've just felt sorry for you. That's no way to live."

She sneered and tightened her hold around Bailey's neck.

"Why'd you have my father killed?" Ed asked.

"He knew information he didn't need to know. It was only after he died we discovered that he had made copies of some very sensitive documents and had hidden them somewhere. And we needed to find it. There are names there. Specific names."

"Bailey doesn't have them," Ed said.

"Ed, they threatened my sister," Bailey tried to explain. If they didn't work together, they were both going to die. She had to get through to him—fast. "I had no choice. Please, Ed. Keeping that from you was killing me."

His gaze flickered toward her. She saw the questions

in his eyes. But she also saw that desire for trust. He had to believe her.

"Killing someone isn't going to accomplish anything right now," Bailey continued. "The CIA will be all over it if we die."

"Not if the right person at the CIA has a say in this," Sanderson said. "Have you ever heard of the term *cover-up*? Some people will do anything to protect their own hides."

Lightning flashed outside and the first smattering of rain hit the glass surrounding them.

"Only unethical people like yourself," Ed muttered.

"Ethics will get you nowhere. You need manipulation, leverage, a little bit of backstabbing. That's how you get places." Claire gave up on choking Bailey and pushed her to the side. "Now, we'll take those letters."

"Don't give them to her, Bailey," Ed warned.

"There's nothing there, Ed," Bailey explained. "They're just kind notes your father wrote to us before he passed."

"My dad didn't write letters like that, Bailey. Claire knows that."

"You mean, we were looking for these letters the whole time? But there was nothing there. I promise." Bailey tried to put the pieces together.

"Sometimes there's more than the eye can see," Ed said.

"That's enough." Sanderson's voice sliced through the air. "Kill her. Kill them both."

Sanderson raised his gun toward Bailey. Before he could shoot, Ed tackled him.

Glass shattered again. Ed and Sanderson flew out the windows and onto the steep roof.

They rolled toward the edge.

Bailey gasped as she glimpsed the men struggling.

But she didn't have too much time to watch.

Because Claire lunged toward her, propelling her into the bench. It crashed behind her, and pain shot through her body.

Ed grabbed the molding near the roof before going over the edge. All of his weight pulled downward, trying to bring all of him with it. As his gun slid down, he reached to grab it but missed. It plummeted to the ground below.

He made the mistake of looking down.

Falling from here could very well mean his death.

He looked up, saw Sanderson pull himself back onto the roof. He stalked over to Ed, glaring down at him with menace in his eyes. He'd retrieved his gun and pointed it at Ed now.

Sanderson's foot crept closer to Ed's fingers. He had to think fast or he'd end up dead, the information would end up in the wrong hands and who knew what would happen with Bailey.

Was she telling the truth? Had they blackmailed her into all of this?

Maybe he hadn't been wrong about her. Maybe she was just as much a victim in all of this as his father had been.

Sanderson's feet crushed his fingers. Ed let out a moan.

"Don't do this, Sanderson!" Ed yelled. The wind tried to carry his voice off.

Another storm was coming, though not as big as the previous one. But if Sanderson didn't kill him out here on the roof, the storm just might. Lightning flashed around him, just looking for the highest point of impact. Ed hoped that wouldn't be this roof.

His fingers began to slip under the strain of Sanderson's weight.

All of a sudden, Sanderson fell onto the roof.

Ed looked up and saw Bailey standing there, part of the bench in her hands. Her hair whipped around her in the wind as she looked down at Ed for a moment.

Ed held his breath. This was the moment. The moment when it would be confirmed what side Bailey was on. In his heart, he thought he knew the answer. But he'd been fooled before...

Suddenly, Bailey was kneeling before him, reaching for his hand. "Let me help you!"

"You're not going to be able to pull me up, Bailey." If anything, he'd end up pulling her down and to her death, as well. He couldn't risk that.

Claire appeared behind Bailey, ready to strike.

"Bailey, watch out!" Ed yelled.

Bailey ducked as the woman swung at her.

Instead, Claire dived toward Bailey and both of them toppled back inside the widow's walk. Moving quickly, Ed pulled himself up. He started toward Bailey when Sanderson suddenly rose. The vengeance in his eyes grew as he lunged toward Ed.

Ed braced himself, knowing that one wrong move could immobilize him. He needed his gun, but that was no longer an option. That left him to defend himself with only the weapons God had given him.

His strength, his training, but mostly his mind.

He heard Bailey cry out inside and jerked his head in her direction. Sanderson took that opportunity to sock him in the jaw.

Ed caught himself before falling to the ground. Sanderson already had the advantage, though. The man was ready to pounce.

Ed's feet began slipping downward as rain pelted the already steep roof.

He eyed Sanderson. Before the man could make a move, Ed dived for the widow's walk. He had to protect Bailey, had to make sure she was okay.

He stood just in time to block Claire's fist before it impacted with Bailey. Claire swung around, catching Ed in a kick.

"Stop right there!" Sanderson said.

Everyone froze and looked up. Sanderson stood there with a gun.

"It's time to finish this," Sanderson said, stepping closer.

His gun was aimed right at Ed.

Ed's pulse spiked. He had to think of a way to get out of this.

He pushed Bailey behind him, knowing that at any minute Sanderson could pull the trigger.

Just then, a gunshot rang out.

Ed froze, waiting to feel pain. Waiting to see blood. Waiting for the fallout.

Bailey watched in horror as Sanderson sank to the ground.

Another gunshot rang out, and Claire moaned before falling against the wall, an unreadable look in her eyes.

A figure stood behind them.

"Henry Wilkins? What are you doing here?" Ed muttered.

Henry lowered the gun in his hands, suddenly not looking as frail as he usually did. "I was taking a walk after my wife went to sleep, you know, just to clear my head. As I was coming past the property, I heard glass shatter and saw the fight up here on the roof. I was coming to help, when I saw Ed's gun fall. So I grabbed it and rushed up. You two okay?"

Bailey nodded, still in shock. "I think…I think so."

Ed grabbed Sanderson's gun and kept it raised toward Claire. Then he turned to Henry. "What…?"

"I was your dad's right-hand man. Certainly you didn't think he kept me on staff because of my brute strength and eye for landscaping?"

Bailey cracked the first hint of a smile she'd had all night. "You're CIA?"

He nodded. "Carter and I went way back. I was only in the agency a few years, but your father asked me to come work for him and be a second set of eyes. I've tried to keep an eye on the two of you since you've been here, as well. Tonight, that was a good thing."

"Why didn't my dad tell me this?" Ed asked.

"He didn't want you to worry. But he needed someone to watch his back down here. He knew I'd moved here, and then he found this house. It just seemed like a natural fit."

Steps sounded on the stairs. A moment later, Sheriff Davis stepped into the widow's walk. His gaze went to the two people on the floor. Both were injured, but Bailey guessed they'd survived. Henry had shot them in the shoulder.

"What's going on up here?" the sheriff demanded.

"It's a long story," Ed said. "But you're going to want to make some phone calls—after you cuff these guys."

TWENTY-THREE

Several hours later, just as dawn was breaking, the police, FBI, CIA and who knew how many other agencies Bailey couldn't identify cleared the house. Sanderson and Claire were both taken into custody and escorted to the hospital. They were expected to survive their injuries, which was a good thing because there was a lot of information the government needed to get from them.

Henry had been taken in for questioning since he was the one who'd pulled the trigger. He was also the one who'd called the sheriff to come out. Meanwhile, Doc Jennings was in town and had agreed to stay with Henry's wife until he returned.

Finally, everything was quiet at the house. Bailey turned toward Ed as they stood in the living room, a fire roaring and coffee in hand.

"I still don't understand what was in those letters that was so important," Bailey began, needing to resolve this case before she thought about anything else. "And all the chemicals, the equipment, the photography lab. None of that makes sense."

Micah had shown up, and he'd taken the letters with him. He wasn't the one who'd visited her sister. It must have been one of Sanderson's men.

"The letters contained microdots," Ed told her, rubbing her arms.

"Microdots?"

Ed nodded. "They're so small they look like a period at the end of a sentence. Yet, when they're examined with the right equipment, there's actually a lot of valuable information located in that small little dot."

"That sounds like something from a spy movie."

"Well, my dad was in the spy business. Some things you see in Hollywood are actually true."

"So your dad was making the microdots using the equipment up in the hayloft?"

Ed nodded. "You've got it. Those microdots had information on Reginald Peterson, the hostage. The proper people at the CIA will be investigated, as well. But the good news is that Sanderson and Claire will be going away and won't be able to hurt anyone else. If they'd gotten their hands on that information, they would have been able to hold it as leverage over high-ranking members of the CIA. It would have been trouble. Big trouble."

"What do you think will happen with Reginald?"

"I think with this information we'll be able to negotiate his release. There are enough agencies involved right now that there's a lot of accountability. No one will be able to get away with anything."

Bailey shifted to face him better. "Ed, I need to explain something to you."

He shook his head. "You don't have to explain."

"I want to. Please. A man—Sanderson, I now know—dragged me into a room that first night you were here. He told me if I didn't find the information that he would kill my sister and her family. I didn't want to risk her life."

"You did the right thing." He hooked a hair behind her ear and put down his coffee mug. "I think you were really brave."

He took her mug from her hands and set it beside his.

Then he turned back to her and cupped her face with his hands.

"I didn't feel brave. I was just trying to survive. And I felt awful the whole time. It's not my personality to hide things like this from people, especially from people I care about."

"You care about me?" Ed asked.

She let out a soft laugh. "You can't tell?"

"That's good. Because I care about you, too." He leaned closer.

Bailey's heart sped and her skin tingled.

His lips just brushed hers when the doorbell rang. They pulled back from each other and let out a nervous laugh.

"Who now?" Ed asked.

"I'm not sure I want to know."

He sighed and, as he let go of her, he almost seemed reluctant to step away. Bailey stayed where she was, part of her conditioned to expect the worst.

No, everyone was behind bars now, she reminded herself. The danger was over and she could relax.

A familiar voice rang through the house and, a moment later, Doc Jennings stepped inside. He tipped his head toward her. "Bailey. Good to see you."

"You, too, Doc. Is everything okay?"

The doctor nodded. "Henry's back and he's with his Florence now. I wanted to stop by and offer you a proposition." He sucked in a deep breath. "Bailey, I'm sure you've heard this already, but I've been thinking about retiring for a while now. I want to move to Texas and be with my grandkids, but I can't leave the island here with no medical personnel. I wondered if you might be willing to fill my shoes."

"I'm no doctor. I couldn't replace you," Bailey insisted.

"No, but you're a nurse. You're a good nurse. You could oversee some of the ailments people around here deal with.

Maybe you could even go back and become a physician's assistant or nurse practitioner. I think you'd do a wonderful job here on the island. It's obvious you love the residents, and they love you."

Bailey glanced at Ed. "I'm flattered. I really am. But I'm going to need to think about it. There are other considerations, after all. Places to live, making enough money to live on."

The doctor nodded. "Of course. Think about it. I'm sure we could work something out."

He nodded toward Ed again and then stepped back. "I'm going to be going now. Let me know what you decide."

When Ed closed the door, he stepped back over to Bailey, picking up right where they'd left off. "What do you think about that?" Ed asked.

"It's something to consider. But there are so many details to think about."

"You could stay here," Ed said, his eyes twinkling.

"At your father's house? Your house now, I suppose."

"Maybe not right away. Maybe you stay at one of your friend Samantha's cabins for a while."

"A while?"

He shrugged. "I've been thinking about a career change for a while now. Maybe I can make Smuggler's Cove my permanent residence."

"And do what?"

"I'm not sure yet. But I'll figure it out."

She crossed her arms. "Practice law?"

He shifted. "About that…"

"Yes?"

"I did go to law school, but I was recruited by the CIA to work for them. I just used the attorney job title as a cover."

"Great. I'm starting to fall in love with a spy."

Ed pulled her closer. "What was that?"

She bit her lip, wishing the words hadn't popped out.

There was no taking them back now, though. "I'm falling in love. It's true."

"I'm glad to hear that, Bailey, because, as crazy as this sounds, I'm falling in love with you, too. I can't imagine my future without you. I really, really want to see where this goes. You and me."

A smile cracked her face. "I like that idea, too."

Ed pulled her close, and his lips covered hers.

EPILOGUE

Two months later

Bailey picked up the platter with the turkey and carried it to the dining room table. She smiled when she stepped into the room. Her smile widened as she heard the TV blaring from the other room, reporting nonstop about the release of hostage Reginald Peterson.

Everyone who was important to her sat at the table. Lauren was here with her kids and her husband, who'd just returned from deployment. They were thriving and, most of all, they were safe.

Henry and his wife had joined them, along with Samantha, John and Connor.

She felt herself beaming when she looked at Ed, though. It was hard to believe that a relationship that had begun with so much distrust had grown into what it was today.

"You need a hand, honey?" he asked, standing.

Bailey shook her head. "I think I'll manage."

She placed the turkey on the table . She wanted to make sure her sister could be here, so she'd postponed the get-together and they were having a late Thanksgiving dinner.

"Before we celebrate everything we have to be thankful for, I wanted to add one more thing to the list," Ed said, addressing the dinner guests. He smiled at Bailey before continuing. "I'm pleased to announce that I asked Bailey to marry me, and I'm just as shocked as anyone that she actually said yes. We'll be getting married at Christmas."

A mixture of laughter and congratulations filled the room.

Bailey couldn't stop herself from grinning as Ed's arm slipped around her waist.

"I just got this nice little job offer with an organization called Eyes," Ed continued. "Their headquarters is down in Virginia Beach, but they've said I can work from home for a majority of the time. They're a paramilitary organization."

John raised his eyebrows, looking impressed as he nodded slowly. "Iron, Incorporated? I've heard mention of them on the news. They only hire the best."

"Yeah, I worked with some of them last year. Apparently, I made an impression."

Henry chuckled. "You have a way of doing that. So, you took the job?"

Ed nodded. "I did. And Bailey has accepted a permanent position as the island nurse."

"It sounds like everything is really coming together for you both," John said.

"This is some house that you guys are going to live in," Lauren said.

"It will be quite the change from the little fishing cabin where you've been staying," Samantha added with a smile. "I'm really happy for you two, though."

Bailey smiled up at Ed. "Me, too."

Ed leaned toward her and whispered, "I love you."

She squeezed his hand, glad the worry from her past was finally over. She knew beyond a doubt that she could trust Ed, not only with her life but with her heart. "I love you, too."

* * * * *

Dear Reader,

Thanks for taking the time to read *Hidden Agenda*. I first introduced Ed Carter in *High-Stakes Holiday Reunion*, and I knew he had to have his own book. There's nothing I love more than a good spy story, and Smuggler's Cove seemed like the perfect setting for Ed and Bailey to meet and eventually fall in love.

During the book, Ed reflected on living a life of transformation instead of simply conforming to everyone around him. There's a lot to be said for living a life that reflects Christ, for being set apart and for allowing Christ's love to change us.

I hope you enjoyed Ed and Bailey's story and your time in Smuggler's Cove.

Blessings,

REQUEST YOUR FREE BOOKS!
2 FREE RIVETING INSPIRATIONAL NOVELS
PLUS 2 FREE MYSTERY GIFTS

Love Inspired® SUSPENSE

YES! Please send me 2 FREE Love Inspired® Suspense novels and my 2 FREE mystery gifts (gifts are worth about $10). After receiving them, if I don't wish to receive any more books, I can return the shipping statement marked "cancel." If I don't cancel, I will receive 4 brand-new novels every month and be billed just $4.74 per book in the U.S. or $5.24 per book in Canada. That's a savings of at least 21% off the cover price. It's quite a bargain! Shipping and handling is just 50¢ per book in the U.S. and 75¢ per book in Canada.* I understand that accepting the 2 free books and gifts places me under no obligation to buy anything. I can always return a shipment and cancel at any time. Even if I never buy another book, the two free books and gifts are mine to keep forever.

123/323 IDN F5AC

Name	(PLEASE PRINT)
Address	Apt. #
City	State/Prov.	Zip/Postal Code

Signature (if under 18, a parent or guardian must sign)

Mail to the Harlequin® Reader Service:
IN U.S.A.: P.O. Box 1867, Buffalo, NY 14240-1867
IN CANADA: P.O. Box 609, Fort Erie, Ontario L2A 5X3

**Are you a current subscriber to Love Inspired Suspense books
and want to receive the larger-print edition?
Call 1-800-873-8635 or visit www.ReaderService.com.**

* Terms and prices subject to change without notice. Prices do not include applicable taxes. Sales tax applicable in N.Y. Canadian residents will be charged applicable taxes. Offer not valid in Quebec. This offer is limited to one order per household. Not valid for current subscribers to Love Inspired Suspense books. All orders subject to credit approval. Credit or debit balances in a customer's account(s) may be offset by any other outstanding balance owed by or to the customer. Please allow 4 to 6 weeks for delivery. Offer available while quantities last.

Your Privacy—The Harlequin® Reader Service is committed to protecting your privacy. Our Privacy Policy is available online at www.ReaderService.com or upon request from the Harlequin Reader Service.
We make a portion of our mailing list available to reputable third parties that offer products we believe may interest you. If you prefer that we not exchange your name with third parties, or if you wish to clarify or modify your communication preferences, please visit us at www.ReaderService.com/consumerschoice or write to us at Harlequin Reader Service Preference Service, P.O. Box 9062, Buffalo, NY 14269. Include your complete name and address.

LIS13R

SPECIAL EXCERPT FROM

Framed for a crime she didn't commit,
museum curator Lana Gomez must prove her
innocence under the watchful eyes of
Capitol K-9 Unit officer Adam Donovan.

Read on for a sneak preview of
the next exciting installment of the
***CAPITOL K-9 UNIT** series,*
DUTY BOUND GUARDIAN
*by **Terri Reed**.*

K-9 officer Adam Donovan's cell buzzed inside the breast pocket of his uniform shirt. He halted, staying out of the rain beneath the overhang covering the entrance to the E. Barrett Prettyman Federal Courthouse.

"Sit," he murmured to his partner, Ace, a four-year-old, dark-coated, sleek Doberman pinscher. The dog obediently sat on his right. Keeping Ace's lead in his left hand, he answered the call. "Adam Donovan."

By habit Adam scanned the crowds of tourists flooding the National Mall, on alert for any criminal activity. Not even nighttime or an April drizzle could keep sightseers in their hotels. To his right the central dome of the US Capitol building gleamed with floodlights, postcard perfect.

"Gavin here" came the deep voice of his boss, Captain Gavin McCord. "You still at the courthouse?"

Adam had had a late meeting with the DA regarding a case against a drug dealer who'd been selling in and around the metro DC area. The elite Capitol K-9 Unit had been called in to assist the local police during a two-hour manhunt nine months ago. The K-9 unit was often enlisted in various crimes throughout the Washington, DC, area.

Ace had been the one to find the suspect hiding in a construction Dumpster outside of the National Gallery of Art. The suspect took the DA's deal and gave up the names of his associates rather than stand trial, which had been scheduled to begin later this week.

A victory on this rainy spring evening.

"Yes, sir."

"There's been a break-in at the American Museum and two of the museum employees have been assaulted," Gavin stated.

"Injured or dead?" Adam asked, already moving down the steps toward his vehicle with Ace at his heels.

"Injured. The intruder rendered both employees unconscious, but the security guard came to and pulled the fire alarm, scaring off the intruder. Both have been rushed to the hospital on Varnum Street." Gavin's tone intensified. "But the other victim is who I'm interested in. Lana Gomez."

Don't miss
DUTY BOUND GUARDIAN by Terri Reed,
available April 2015 wherever
Love Inspired® Suspense books and ebooks are sold.

www.Harlequin.com